Megan Sparks

Roller Girls

Megan Sparks

Roller Girls

Boot Camp Blues

With special thanks to Lisa Fiedler

First published in 2013 by Curious Fox,
an imprint of Capstone Global Library Limited,
7 Pilgrim Street, London, EC4V 6LB
Registered company number: 6695582

www.curious-fox.com

Text © Hothouse Fiction Ltd 2013

Series created by Hothouse Fiction
www.hothousefiction.com

The author's moral rights are hereby asserted.

Cover designed by Jo Hinton-Malivoire, original concept by
www.spikyshooz.com
Illustrations by Allan Campbell

ISBN 978 1 78202 035 6

1 3 5 7 9 10 8 6 4 2

A CIP catalogue for this book is available from the British Library.

Print... ...4YY

www.fsc.org   FSC C020471

For my Coffee Club girls – Margaret, Mary and Corrinne. When life has me skating in circles, you're always there to help keep me on my feet!

Chapter One

To Annie, Liberty Heights seemed to be melting into a huge grey puddle.

Everything that had been so lovely about the Illinois winter – those crisp blue skies and the blankets of pure white snow – was now morphing into a slushy, drab mess. Even walking home from high school along the pleasant Main Street felt dreary and bone-chilling.

"Ugh," Annie muttered, stepping over an icy patch. "How long until spring?"

Her best friend, Lexie, laughed. "Forever. Or at least that's how it always feels at this time of the year."

Annie felt a twinge of homesickness. That didn't happen much any more. After living there for five months, she thought of Liberty Heights as home now, but this bleak day had her longing for the early spring warmth of London, where she'd grown up. Hyde Park was probably already carpeted in daffodils. She pictured her mum in the tiny garden of their flat in Kensington, coaxing the newborn crocuses out of the earth.

OK, so Mum had never been much of a crocus coaxer (she was a workaholic lawyer – far too busy for hobbies like gardening) but it was still a nice image.

They covered their heads with their hands as they passed under a jagged row of icicles that dripped from a roof edge. "February can be a real drag," said Lexie.

"Yeah," Annie grumbled, taking in the paper hearts that decorated the windows of the Main Street shops. "For lots of reasons."

Not long ago, she'd been dating Tyler Erickson, the captain of the soccer team and the coolest boy in school. At first, she'd thought he was perfect, but as their relationship went on, she came to realize that other than gorgeous green eyes, a hot body, and a killer smile, Tyler had little to offer. He hadn't been supportive – not when it really mattered – and the relationship had ended badly. Annie was pretty much over Tyler, but now that the whole world seemed obsessed with Cupid, she couldn't help wishing she had a valentine. Someone to send her flowers or share a romantic dinner with…

No! Annie shook her head. She refused to let the fact that Valentine's Day was coming up get her down. Grim weather and romantic greetings card occasions aside, Annie really loved living here in Liberty Heights.

It had been almost six months since her parents' separation, the event that had prompted Annie's dad to return to his hometown in America. He'd decided to open a British-style tea room in Liberty Heights. Some people were surprised that Annie chose to go with her father instead of staying in London with her mother. It wasn't that Annie didn't love her mum; she'd always been proud of Philippa's work ethic and her success as a lawyer. It was just that Dad had always been the stay-at-home parent – the one who drove Annie to gymnastics, cooked dinner, and put the cold compresses on her forehead when she had a fever. So it just seemed natural to go with him and support him as he pursued his dream. The first weeks had been difficult, and she still missed her mum, but for the most part, Annie didn't regret moving at all.

She'd made a brilliant best friend in Lexie, who was funny, artistic, and totally unconventional. Dad's café, Rosie Lee's, was thriving, and Annie was really getting the hang of being an American teenager. Not a typical one, though … not by a long shot.

Because Annie was a roller girl! She'd discovered her local roller derby team early on and hadn't looked back. When she was playing derby she felt like she was right where she belonged. So what if some kids at school thought roller derby wasn't a real sport, and considered the people who played it freaks? Annie loved it and that was all that mattered.

The girls had reached Rosie Lee's now. Even from the

pavement Annie could smell the delicious aromas of pies baking and coffee brewing. But today, Annie would have preferred staying outside in the freezing gloom.

"Oh, c'mon," Lexie said, reading Annie's mind as she pulled open the door. "It'll be fun."

"That's easy for you to say," Annie said. "You'll be the one *behind* the camera!"

"And you'll be the pretty face in the newspaper ad," Lexie reminded her. "Just pretend it's a professional photo shoot and that you're a famous supermodel."

Annie's dad was planning to run a Valentine's-Day-themed advertisement in the *Liberty Heights Gazette* and he'd asked Annie and Lexie to help him out. Annie would be featured in the ad, and Lexie, with her artistic eye, would photograph it.

Together, Lexie and Dad had put together an idea for the advert, including some elaborate costuming, designed and sewn by Lexie. Unfortunately, they'd kept it all a secret from Annie. They'd called it a "surprise" but Annie was wary. Knowing Dad and Lexie, this was going to be something crazy and over the top, and they'd probably decided that keeping the details from her would be the only way to get Annie to do it.

"I had my mom drop off the costumes this morning," Lexie explained, nudging Annie through the door.

"Sometimes having a super-creative best friend has its drawbacks," Annie said. "Just tell me this ... is it worse than the Queen Elizabeth outfit Dad made me wear at the grand opening of Rosie Lee's?"

"Oh, it's way better!" Lexie said, giggling.

Somehow, that did little to reassure Annie. Lexie went over to the coat pegs and removed an oversized garment bag, but before she could unveil Annie's costume, Dad came bustling out of the kitchen. He was dressed up like … the jack in a deck of playing cards?

"Oh, no!" Annie covered her eyes with her hands. "Please tell me this isn't happening."

"He's the Knave of Hearts!" Lexie announced proudly. "You know, from *Alice in Wonderland*."

"Hearts," Dad repeated, pointing to the giant red felt heart sewn onto the front of his white satin tunic. "For Valentine's Day. Get it?"

"Yes, Dad. I get it." Annie sighed, eyeing his outfit. He wore a ridiculous blond pageboy wig, with a floppy red satin hat perched on top. The white tunic flowed down to – oh, no! – a pair of pantaloons and glittery tights! On his feet were red felt slippers with pointy toes that curled up.

Annie had the fleeting thought that she might be able to borrow those tights to wear to a derby bout. Then it hit her. "Woah. If you're the Knave of Hearts, then I'm going to be—"

"Ta da!" cried Lexie, tugging the bag off the hanger to reveal the costume.

Annie actually gasped.

"Your gown, Your Majesty," said Dad, sweeping into a low bow. "A dress fit for the Queen of Hearts."

Lexie was beaming as she held up her handiwork. Annie had

to admit it was fabulous, with its black sequined bodice, dotted with glittery hearts. The puffed sleeves were red and white striped and the red satin skirt billowed out like a huge bell. A red velvet cape trimmed with faux fur and a jewelled crown finished off the ensemble.

"It's amazing," said Annie, trying to sound enthusiastic. She knew Lexie must have spent hours designing and sewing this masterpiece. But wearing it in the newspaper for all to see? That was a terrifying proposition. Since splitting up with Tyler, Annie had been trying to keep a low profile. And this was definitely not the dress to do it in.

"Righty-o, ladies," said Dad, putting on his ridiculous cockney accent as he placed a plate of freshly baked goodies on a table. "Take a moment to sample me luverly wares. Then we'll knuckle down." He turned to smile at Lexie. "A cup of coffee for our stylist-slash-photographer?"

"Yes, please."

"Can I have a cup of tea?" asked Annie, sinking into a chair.

"What else is new?" Lexie giggled. "I guess you can take the girl out of England, but you can't take England out of the girl."

Annie gave her friend a small smile and reached for one of the treats. Dad had baked heart-shaped tarts filled with tangy berry jam. One bite went a long way towards taking her mind off her newspaper appearance. "These are delicious, Dad."

"They really are, Mr Turner," Lexie agreed, tasting one.

"Save some for the shoot," said Dad, returning with the hot drinks. "And the customers!" The girls took a moment to enjoy their snack as a handful of customers came and went. Dad told each of them to keep an eye out for his advert in the weekend *Gazette*; he promised there would be a coupon for Valentine's treats.

Wonderful, thought Annie, imagining people gawking at her in the Queen of Hearts costume. And the worst part was that on Valentine's Day, she wasn't going to be the queen of *anyone's* heart.

Several minutes later, she was dressed in the red and black gown, which reached the floor even though Annie was five foot eleven and a half. She'd pulled her long, brown hair into a loose bun and Lexie had done her eyes in sparkly silver shadow. Annie had coloured her lips with dark red lipstick to create a haughty pout. All in all, she was happy to see she looked more glamorous than ridiculous.

Lexie posed them with a giant tray of tarts, ordering Dad to pretend to steal them, and telling Annie to give him her best "Off with your head!" look. Things got silly, with Dad stuffing three whole tarts into his mouth at once, and Annie posing dramatically with her hand pressed to her forehead as if it was all just too much to bear.

Lexie snapped shot after shot, laughing the whole time.

"If you two ever get tired of running a café," she said finally, "you've both got a real future in theatre."

Laughing, Annie removed her crown and checked the teapot-shaped clock on the wall.

"I've got to go," she said. "Derby practice. Dad, can I have a lift?"

"Anything for the Queen of Hearts," said Dad.

For a brief moment, Annie thought her dad was planning to drive her to the roller rink in his costume. And since there was always a fifty-fifty chance of their ailing truck breaking down, she panicked. She could only imagine what people would think if they saw the Knave of Hearts walking to the nearest petrol station.

Luckily, when she came out of the toilets dressed for derby, she saw that Dad had also changed back into his normal clothes.

Dad locked up, and they headed out to the truck.

"Lexie, can I drop you off on the way?" Dad offered, turning the key. The old pickup started with a horrible screeching sound.

"No thanks," said Lexie, grimacing at the noise. "I think I've got a better chance of making it home on foot."

Dad laughed and nodded. "I really need to get it into the garage to see about the fan belt. But I've been sort of pressed for time."

And money, Annie added silently, slipping into the passenger seat. Even though Rosie Lee's was doing a steady trade, the cost of starting it up had been high. Annie and her dad were far from destitute, but it was going to be a while before they could breathe easily when it came to unexpected spending.

"Thanks for all your help," she called out of the window to Lexie.

Then she covered her ears as Dad put the truck into drive.

Chapter Two

Dad dropped Annie at the rink entrance.

"You wanna come in and watch practice for a bit?" Annie offered. "This is going to be the last one for a while."

This thought sent a stab of sadness right to Annie's heart. Technically, the season was over – and the Liberty Belles had won the league championships! But on the downside, Annie and the girls would be derby-free until the autumn. Today's practice was a special one, called by Coach Ritter so the girls could get in one last workout, clear out their lockers, and say goodbye.

"I'd love to," said Dad, "but I don't think that would be advisable. I'm afraid if I turn off the motor, I'll never get it going again."

"I'll get a ride home from Lauren's mum," Annie said.

"Good thinking." Dad laughed, then waved and drove off. The truck growled menacingly.

Just as Annie reached the glass entrance door, she heard a familiar whirring sound. She turned to see Jesse, bundled into a thick hoodie and heavy gloves, his black hair hidden under a beanie, rolling up on his skateboard.

He smiled at Annie as Dad pulled out of the car park.

"That noise can only mean one of two things," he said, hopping off the board and flipping it up into his hand. "Either Godzilla has arrived to devour Liberty Heights or your Dad's pickup is in serious need of a fan belt. I almost couldn't hear the Nirvana CD he was blasting."

Annie giggled. "OK, first of all, the Nirvana CD is mine. And second of all, you're right. It's pretty clear that our poor old fan belt might have to be put out of its misery."

Jesse laughed. "Sad but true." He opened the door to the rink and held it for Annie. "If you want, I can take a look at it."

"Really? You know about trucks?"

"I know about anything with wheels. Skates, skateboards, bikes, cars. I'm *that* guy."

"Ah, well, if *that guy* could possibly fix our fan belt, we'd be very grateful. Thanks, Jesse."

As Annie headed for the locker room, she thought about how thoughtful and sweet Jesse was. If she'd ever told Tyler her dad's truck needed attention, he wouldn't have cared.

Stop thinking about Tyler; he's a big jerk.

In the locker room, Lauren, Sharmila, Holly, Carmen, Liz,

and the other Liberty Belles were getting into their gear.

"So, Lauren," Holly teased, "I saw you talking to a cute sophomore guy outside the chemistry lab this morning. Looked like some major valentine potential."

Lauren gave an awkward laugh. "We were just talking about homework."

"Yeah, right," said Sharmila, waggling her eyebrows. "There was more chemistry happening between you two than there was in the lab!"

Lauren just ducked her head and focused on putting on her skates.

"Guess who I saw at the mall this afternoon," said Carmen. "Kelsey. She was making a big deal about buying these stupid boxer shorts for her new boyfriend as a Valentine's Day gift."

At that, the entire locker room went silent and all eyes shot to Annie, who felt her stomach flip over.

Carmen frowned and looked from one grim face to another. "What? What did I say?"

"Kelsey's *new* boyfriend is Annie's *old* one," Liz whispered.

Carmen immediately went pale. "OMG, Annie. I'm so sorry. I had no idea she and Tyler were going out together."

Annie shrugged. "It's OK. How could you know? They just started dating, like, five minutes ago." *Of course, Tyler and I only broke up, like, six minutes ago.*

Truth be told, the fact that Tyler was suddenly all up in Kelsey's pom-poms did kind of sting. Annie's history with the head cheerleader, Kelsey, was not a good one. Ever since Annie had turned down a spot on the cheerleading squad, Kelsey had made it her personal mission to make Annie's life difficult.

"Besides," Annie said, forcing a carefree smile, "I'm completely over him. And completely over Valentine's Day. I'm boycotting it this year."

Lauren laughed. "Boycotting Valentine's Day. I love it."

"Well, I don't," said Sharmila, just as Coach Ritter entered the locker room. "I like the idea of some hot guy buying me chocolate and swooning over me, even if it does only happen one day of the year."

"Guys swoon over you all the time," Holly reminded her.

Sharmila struck a pose and fluffed her hair. "True."

Everyone laughed, even Annie. Sharmila had the looks of a Bollywood star, with her long black hair and striking green eyes.

"Well I'm certainly not looking forward to baking two dozen heart-shaped cookies for my daughter's class Valentine Day's party and helping Abby make twenty-four cards for her classmates," Coach said.

"Why don't you order the cookies from Annie's dad?" Carmen suggested. "The ones he baked for our Christmas party were awesome."

"I'm sure he'll give you a derby discount," Lauren added, "since you're Annie's coach and all."

Annie smiled. She was sure Dad would be glad to help out Coach Ritter, but it had less to do with her being the coach and more to do with the fact that he had a pretty huge crush on her. They'd been out on a couple of dates, and Annie had even seen them kiss under the mistletoe back in December.

"I'll place the order for you when I get home tonight," Annie said.

"Thanks," said Coach, visibly relieved. "Well, now that I don't have to worry about cookies, what do you say we get on with practice? Remember, girls, it is really important to stay fit in the off season, so you're in shape when next season starts."

"I know," said Holly, sadly. "But it is more fun to work out as a team."

The others nodded their agreement. None of them were looking forward to a derby hiatus.

"Hey, I have an idea," said Liz, the team captain, as the girls made their way out of the locker room. "Let's have an anti-Valentine's Day *bout*! We can hold it on the fourteenth and take out all our romantic frustrations on the track!"

"I love that idea!" cried Lauren.

"Me too," said Annie, thrilled at the prospect of more derby time. "Let's do it."

"Um…" Sharmila looked worried. "What if we don't have any romantic frustrations? In other words, what if we already have a date for Valentine's Day?"

Annie felt that familiar twinge of envy for the stunning Sharmila. Of course she'd have a date for the most romantic night of the year. For all Annie knew, Sharmila had had to choose between ten different guys, all begging to take her out.

Liz laughed. "That's OK. It'll just be an exhibition. No one will be penalized for missing it. It's short notice, so we can't expect everyone to be available."

Annie groaned. She was available. She was so available it hurt. But the thought of being with the Liberty Belles on Valentine's Day was actually extremely comforting.

"No dates, just skates!" Annie quipped and everyone cracked up.

"I bet we can get the High Rollers to jump on board," said Carmen. "They're always up for a scrimmage."

"I'll set it up," said Coach. "Now, in keeping with our anti-Valentine's Day theme, let's do a drill called Breaking Up is Hard to Do."

Don't I know it, thought Annie with a sigh, but she had to admit, she did feel much better than she had before Liz suggested the exhibition bout.

"Isn't that the title of an old song?" asked Lauren.

Coach smiled, then snapped her fingers and as if by magic, the rink was filled with the sounds of Neil Sedaka's classic "Breaking Up is Hard to Do".

The magic, of course, was Jesse. Clearly, Coach had arranged in advance for him to have this song cued up on the sound system. Since Annie and Jesse shared a love of punk and alternative music, she wondered if it was killing him to play such a cheesy old song. But then again, he was always willing to play music that was in keeping with the theme of the bout or the season.

The drill called for the Liberty Belles to be divided into groups of three. Two of them would become a wall while the third attempted to break through. Annie found herself paired with Sharmila and Lauren.

"Let's go, wife!" cried Annie, referring to their status as "derby wives", a term meaning they were best derby friends, who always had each other's back. She linked arms with Lauren and put on a mock scowl. "Let's see if Sharmila has what it takes to be a homewrecker!"

"I'll take that as a challenge!" Sharmila said, and set about trying to get through their barrier.

Annie was tall and thin − one of the fastest skaters on the team. Lauren, on the other hand, was short and solidly built, making her a natural blocker. Their opposite strengths made them a great team. But eventually Sharmila managed to break through.

"Now you be the heartbreaker," Annie told Lauren, holding out her arm for Sharmila to take.

"Somebody call a divorce lawyer!" Lauren laughed. "I'm gonna break you two up so bad you'll wish you had a pre-nup!"

Lauren's joke sent a twinge of pain to Annie's heart. Her parents' separation was in the process of becoming a divorce. But she knew Lauren hadn't meant to be insensitive.

Annie and Sharmila sped around the track, sticking together like glue, while Lauren chased after them. They were much faster skaters than their pursuer, but Lauren refused to give up. After a few laps she managed to catch up and burst through the "happy couple".

Then it was Annie's turn to be "the other woman", as Sharmila laughingly put it.

21

Lauren's strength and determination made the two-person wall incredibly strong and Annie's first two attempts were unsuccessful. On her third try, she slammed through.

"Yessss!" cried Annie, pumping the air with her fist. Feeling triumphant, she caught Jesse's eye. He gave her the thumbs up.

A spiral of warmth began in her chest and spread outward, giving her a cosy feeling. She felt so welcome here, so appreciated and, well ... loved. Not that Jesse was in love with her or anything remotely like that. But he was a good friend – like her teammates, he was always looking out for her.

Any residual gloom she'd been feeling about Valentine's Day was gone. Heading back to the lockers, Annie understood now more than ever that there was nothing better than roller derby to take your mind off being single on the fourteenth of February.

"Coach wants to have a quick meeting before we leave," said Liz, hoisting her skate bag onto her shoulder.

"Are we in trouble?" asked Holly, nervously twisting a lock of her crimson-dyed hair.

"I don't think so. She said she has an announcement."

"Maybe she's come up with more ideas for the Valentine's Day bout," said Annie. Costumes, maybe, like they wore on Halloween? Or maybe Coach was going to suggest that they make boy-shaped effigies to burn, like on Guy Fawkes Night back in England. Annie had to giggle at that image, even if it was a little violent.

Coach was waiting for them near the exit.

"I know you guys are bummed that the league season is over," she said. "But the good news is that doesn't necessarily mean that you can't play roller derby until next season. I've just had funding approved to put together a Liberty Heights All-Star team!"

A murmur of excitement rippled through the group.

"I like the sound of that," said Holly, who was one of the most talented of all the roller girls.

"I thought you might," said Coach with a grin. "Here's how it works. I'll hold a formal try-out right after February vacation. It will be open to all four teams in the league: the High Rollers, the Derby Dolls, the Prairie Girls, and of course you Liberty Belles. I'll select a team of the twenty best roller girls in the league to make up the All-Star roster."

"Who will we play against?" asked Lauren.

"All-Star teams from all over the region," Coach explained. "Sometimes we'll have actual bouts, others will be exhibitions. Maybe we'll even lead workshops for younger girls."

"We'll get to travel!" cried Sharmila. "That sounds amazing!"

"If you're interested in trying out, we'll keep having practices between now and try-outs. I'll be watching you very carefully. Every time you take to the track, you'll be under consideration. Everything matters: skills, sportsmanship, willingness to take criticism. I'll add these observations to your performance at the try-out. If we're going to represent our region as All-Stars, I want only the best, most devoted girls on the team."

23

"I am so totally trying out for the All-Star team," Holly announced.

"Me too," said Annie, and Lauren nodded her agreement.

"I wish I could," said Liz. "But I'm already so strapped with school and college prep stuff. I was going to use the spring to catch up on everything."

"Same here," sighed Carmen. "I mean, I'd love to be on the All-Star team, but I was thinking I'd pull some extra shifts at my folks' dry-cleaning shop. I really want to save up to buy a car."

"That's fine, girls," Coach Ritter said. "You're welcome to come to practices anyway, if you just want to work out."

Annie understood that the older girls had other commitments besides roller derby, but couldn't help feeling disappointed that if she made the All-Star team, some of her Liberty Belles teammates wouldn't be a part of it. Of course the likelihood of her even making the elite team was pretty slim; she was only a rookie after all. Still, Annie was determined to work extra hard between now and the try-out. She'd come such a long way in a short time, there was no reason not to have hope.

As she followed Lauren out to her mum's car, Annie felt a rush of excitement. The anti-Valentine's Day bout (even without a flaming effigy of Tyler!) would have been great on its own, but now, with the news about the All-Star team, she felt even better.

She'd been wondering what she would do all spring and summer without derby to keep her busy.

Now she had a goal: to make the All-Star team and keep on skating!

Chapter Three

Lexie came bounding down the hallway and skidded to a halt at Annie's locker. Today, she was rocking a 1960s Motown girl-group look, with her frizzy brown hair smoothed into a "groovy" flip and huge hoop earrings.

"Nice go-go boots," said Annie, grinning.

"Thanks. They were my grandma's during the Summer of Love, if you can believe it." Lexie opened her backpack and pulled out a pile of photos. "But these boots are nothing compared to the pictures I took yesterday! Check 'em out!"

Annie took the photos. There she was, the Queen of Hearts, looking regal and ridiculous at the same time. In one of the shots, Dad's cheeks were puffed out with a mouthful of stolen tarts. But she had to admit, the photographs were brilliant. And if this humorous advert – with a headline that read "EAT YOUR HEART OUT AT ROSIE LEE'S" – didn't bring customers into the shop, nothing would.

"You never cease to amaze me," said Annie, handing Lexie back the photos. "These look professional. You're the most talented person I know."

"Thanks," Lexie said modestly. "Do you think your dad will like them?"

"He'll love them," said Annie. "The sillier I look, the happier he is."

"I think you look awesome," said Lexie, pointing to one of the photos. "I mean, sure, it's supposed to be funny. But you look really good."

The warning bell rang and Annie felt her heart sink. When Lexie noticed the look on her friend's face she gave her a sympathetic smile.

"English this period?"

Annie nodded. Ms Schwarz's literature class used to be her favourite. Now, though, she positively dreaded it.

"Maybe Tyler will ditch class today," Lexie offered.

"Not likely. Athletes can get kicked off the team if they get caught skiving. Tyler may not care about Jane Austen, but soccer is his life."

"So ignore him," Lexie advised, as they walked down the hall together. "That shouldn't be hard to do. The boy's got the personality of a dirty sock."

Annie laughed. "True. Unfortunately, Kelsey is also in the

class and she loves rubbing it in my face that she and Tyler are together now."

"Well, maybe you should remind her that you had him first and didn't want him."

Annie wished she had the guts to be able to do that. She'd stood up to Kelsey before. But seeing Tyler and Kelsey all over each other had a way of draining Annie's confidence.

"Besides," Lexie said, giving Annie a playful elbow to the ribs as they reached Ms Schwarz's classroom. "Kelsey's just the head cheerleader. You're the Queen of Hearts. There's no contest!"

Annie laughed, then took a deep breath and entered her English classroom.

Annie slipped into a desk in the back corner of the room. Before their break-up, Tyler had sat in the seat directly in front of her, but now he'd got into the habit of sitting next to Kelsey.

She took her paperback copy of Austen's *Sense and Sensibility* out of her backpack and began to flip through it. This was Annie's third time reading the book – she'd loved it since reading it in Year Eight, even though it had been a little difficult to get through back then. She'd watched the film to help her understand the more complicated plot points.

Having just gone through a break-up herself, Annie could thoroughly relate to the story. The Dashwood sisters had both been unlucky in love, and their heartache resonated with Annie now in a way it never had before. She opened her notebook and looked at some of the things she'd jotted down as she was re-reading the novel. Her first not-so-academic observation was written in big, bold bubble letters:

GUYS SUCK!!!
IN EVERY CENTURY!!!

Annie wondered if Ms Schwarz would give her an A if she wrote that on their next test. Probably not.

The class bell rang, and for a moment, Annie thought she might be spared the presence of Liberty Heights High's golden couple. But two seconds after the bell Tyler and Kelsey sauntered in, arm in arm. From her desk, Ms Schwarz gave them a sharp look.

But they were both so besotted with each other they didn't even notice the teacher's glare. They remained entwined as they made their way to their desks. When Kelsey finally had to let go of Tyler's hand to take her seat, she looked so devastated you'd think she'd just been taken off life support!

Annie let out a little snort of disgust.

"Now that we're all present and accounted for," Ms Schwarz said, "I'd like to try something a little different today. I'm going to assign you each a partner, which will give us a dozen co-ed pairs."

"I pick Tyler," Kelsey cooed, giving her boyfriend a flirtatious wink.

"Nice try," said the teacher. "But I can't imagine you and Mr Erickson would accomplish much. I don't give extra credit for cuddling."

The whole class (except Annie) cracked up at that. Kelsey didn't even have the decency to blush. If anything, she looked pleased with Ms Schwarz's remark.

When the laughter calmed down, the teacher went about breaking up the class into boy–girl pairs. Kelsey got matched with the boy Annie had been hoping to be paired with – a softly spoken but cute guy named Michael O'Connor, who was the star of the swimming team. This didn't seem to bother Tyler; he was so cocky it probably didn't even occur to him to feel jealous. Annie's derby friend, Tessa, got paired with a boy from the marching band named Charles, who had twinkling blue eyes and seemed to have a great sense of humour. As the teacher went down the class list randomly pairing up girls and boys, Annie began to feel a knot forming in the pit of her stomach. There were only so many possible partners, after all.

Annie felt her chest tightening. Could Annie be unlucky enough to be paired with the one boy in class she couldn't bear to look at, let alone work with?

Ben DeMarco with Emma-Kate McNeely…

Process of elimination was definitely not working in Annie's favour. She held her breath.

"Annie Turner," said Ms Schwarz, "you'll be working with Demetri Vangelis."

A flood of relief washed over Annie.

Demetri raised his hand. "I've got an early dismissal pass," he said. "My mom's picking me up in five minutes for a dentist appointment."

Ms Schwarz sighed. "I sincerely wish you children could see to your dental hygiene on your own time." She ran her pencil over the list again. "Very well. Annie, you can work with Tyler Erickson."

It was all Annie could do to keep from leaping to her feet and screaming, '*Nooooo!*' at the top of her lungs. She hazarded a glance at Kelsey who looked ready to explode.

Tyler merely looked amused.

Oh! *So* cocky!

Annie *refused* to be the one to get up and move to *his* desk. He could collect his books and come to *her*!

She waited as the rest of the students gathered up their belongings and shuffled around the classroom to join their partners. Swimmer Mike wasted no time getting himself over to Kelsey's desk. Even shy Charles had enough gentlemanly courtesy to approach Tessa. But Tyler remained right where he was, looking smug. Annie's foot tapped nervously under the desk, her fingers gripping the novel so tightly her knuckles were white.

"Mr Erickson," Ms Schwarz prompted at last, "your partner is waiting."

With an arrogant look, Tyler picked up his books and strolled across the room towards Annie. He took the seat in front of hers – the one he used to sit in back when they were a couple – and turned his back to the class to face her.

Annie was gritting her teeth so furiously she was afraid she might find herself joining Demetri at the dentist.

But now that Tyler was in front of her, she could see that he was looking a lot less sure of himself. Was it her imagination or did he look as uncomfortable as she did?

"Hi," she mumbled, not fully meeting his eyes.

"Hi."

OK, now what? Annie wondered if congratulating him on his new relationship would seem mature, or snarky. Should she tell him straight out she was over him? Maybe she should just comment on the weather. It wasn't helping that he had on the same shirt he was wearing the first time he'd ever kissed her.

Thankfully, Ms Schwarz picked that moment to explain the assignment.

"The purpose of this exercise is to discuss the relationship, such as it was, between Marianne Dashwood and John Willoughby. The question at the centre or your discourse should be this: did Willoughby really love Marianne, or was he just using her?"

"Let me guess," joked Charles. "The boys are supposed to argue in favour of Willoughby."

"Actually," said Ms Schwarz with a sly grin, "I want to mix things up a bit and have the girls take Willoughby's side."

"You're kidding!" cried Nicole.

"That's impossible," Allison agreed. "Willoughby was a complete jerk!"

"And how can a guy argue for Marianne?" David asked. "She was so blinded by romance she was delusional!"

"The chick was practically a stalker!" Alex added.

"I'm glad I'm leaving early," Demetri remarked, scooping up his books and heading for the door. "My filling is going to be a cakewalk compared to this."

When he was gone, Ms Schwarz continued with her

instructions. "The point is for you to think beyond commonly held gender prejudices and try to imagine how a character of the opposite sex might defend his or her actions. You should take notes on your conversation, and for tonight's homework, I want two paragraphs on what you learned from the discussion."

Everyone grumbled, but after a moment or two, the class got to work.

Annie opened her book and went directly to the scene where Marianne and Willoughby first meet after she twists her ankle and is unable to walk home. The passage reminded her of the sprained ankle she'd suffered last autumn, although the circumstances were far less romantic. She'd been knocked down by her derby nemesis, Dee Stroyer, and, unfortunately, no one had ridden up on a stallion to rescue her.

"Well," said Annie hesitantly, "I suppose Willoughby should get some credit for rescuing Marianne."

Tyler shrugged. "I guess."

Annie cleared her throat. "And it absolutely was not his fault that she fell for him so hard. He couldn't help the fact that he was gorgeous."

"Maybe not," said Tyler. "But he didn't have to lead her on the way he did."

Annie frowned, feeling defensive on the fictional character's behalf. "Maybe he was just being nice."

"Nice?" Tyler gave a wave of his hand. "Guys like Willoughby aren't nice. They have an agenda. And his agenda was to get with Marianne."

"Well, she certainly encouraged him! And remember – he never asked her to marry him. She just assumed—"

"Of course she did! She was young and inexperienced."

"Maybe he loved her back," said Annie. "Maybe in his own way, he did the best he could."

Tyler shook his head and sneered. "His best wasn't good enough, then. And in the end, he took advantage of her." Tyler's green eyes suddenly seemed to deepen, and his voice sounded sincere. "Think about it, Annie. They were from two totally different worlds. Their relationship was doomed from the start. Marianne was too innocent to realize that, so it was up to Willoughby to do the right thing. But he didn't."

"That doesn't mean he didn't love her," Annie countered. "Maybe he was torn between his world and hers."

Tyler mulled this over for a moment, then slumped in his chair and frowned. "OK. So maybe he did, ya know, care about her. A lot. Still, he should have known better than to get involved with a sweet girl like y—" He looked away quickly, catching himself. "Like *her*," he finished quietly.

Annie blinked. Had Tyler just apologized? And had she admitted that maybe part of what went wrong between them had been her fault, too?

It was true – she and Tyler were from opposite worlds, just like Willoughby and Marianne Dashwood. But there was no denying there'd been an attraction, maybe even some real affection. It hadn't worked out, but maybe they could get past the anger, past the blame.

Maybe they could be friends after all.

She was about to offer him a genuine smile when she noticed Kelsey glaring at them from across the room.

Tyler noticed too. He immediately sat up straight and gave Annie a cool look. "The thing is, this is just a stupid assignment and *Sense and Sensibility* is fiction. In real life, any normal guy would have done exactly what Willoughby did." He gave Annie a smirk. "The girl was a waste of his time. Any real guy would forget about her and move on in a second."

The words were like a bucket of cold water tossed in Annie's face.

So much for apologies.

"Well, I guess you would know," she said bitterly, slamming her book shut. "By the way, did you read the whole book?"

"No. Why?"

Annie looked pointedly at Kelsey, who was now openly flirting with Mike. "Let's just say that Willoughby gets exactly what he deserves," Annie snapped, referring to Willoughby's unhappy marriage at the end of *Sense and Sensibility*. With that, she got up and stormed out of the classroom just as the bell rang.

Chapter Four

The rest of the day went by in an angry blur. Annie was barely able to focus on her schoolwork – the ugly scene with Tyler kept floating into her mind and riling her up all over again.

By her last class she was counting the minutes until derby practice because she knew the exercise would shake her out of her miserable mood. Thank goodness Coach Ritter had arranged extra practices, or else she'd be heading home to brood. She needed to vent about Tyler, and she knew her teammates would listen and understand.

Boy, was she wrong!

The normally supportive atmosphere at the rink could be summed up in one phrase: CUT-THROAT.

Five minutes into practice it became clear to Annie that the mindset of the Liberty Belles – who'd been working together like a well-oiled machine for the last several months – had shifted dramatically. They were no longer acting like a united team.

Overnight, they'd gone from being collaborators to being competitors.

Fierce ones!

"Ouch!" Annie let out a grunt as she landed on her bum, hitting the track hard. Lauren had darted out in front of her in an over-enthusiastic block, causing Annie to lose her balance.

"Sorry," called Lauren, not hanging around long enough to offer Annie a hand up.

Coach set them a familiar warm-up drill – Bus Stop – which should have been easy. But today it was a nightmare. Holly seemed to be trying to break the world record for speed on skates and Lauren's actions redefined the term aggressive.

Annie was no fool; she knew exactly what was going on. Since Coach's announcement about the All-Star team, each girl felt it necessary to prove herself. Teammates were now opponents, for any girl who wanted to win a place on the team.

"Well," huffed Coach, "since you all seem determined to clobber each other, we might as well put that to good use. How about a scrimmage?"

Annie looked around the rink. "Against whom? We're the only team here."

"Against yourselves," Coach said.

Annie was put on the same team as Holly, which was a plus, since it meant they wouldn't be jamming against each other.

It was also a minus because Holly was a more experienced jammer than Annie and would probably get more track time because of it.

But to Annie's surprise, Coach chose Annie to be the starting jammer. It was clear that Holly saw this as a slight and Annie could see the slow burn beginning in her eyes.

Holly wasted no time showing off her blocking techniques. Though petite, she was nearly as talented a blocker as she was a jammer and she clearly wanted everyone to remember that. But Annie wasn't there to admire Holly's ability – she had a job to do.

She was in top form, breaking through the pack, then skating swiftly around the track and coming up to the pack again. But when the opportunity arose for Holly to whip Annie forward – a technique that could help their team score – Holly refused to play her part.

Annie glided up to Holly and extended her hand, expecting Holly to grasp it and then use her strength to propel Annie forward.

But Holly ignored Annie's hand as if it wasn't there.

"Hey!" cried Annie, waving her hand in case Holly hadn't recognized her intent. "Whip me!"

Holly kept her eyes straight ahead, leaning into the curve.

"Holly!" Annie shouted again. But the opportunity was lost and the jammer for the other team, Carmen, broke through the pack and scored four points.

Oh, come on! thought Annie.

Carmen patted her hips to call off the jam, and Annie

immediately spun into a toe stop, glaring at Holly.

"What the hell was *that*?" Annie hissed, folding her arms hard across her chest.

Holly shrugged. "Why should I make you look good in front of Coach? There are only so many spots on that All-Star team roster. It's every roller girl for herself now."

"Since when?" Annie demanded. "We've never played with that attitude before. Teamwork is one of the driving forces of derby. It's why we love it."

"Maybe so," Holly said, "but right now what I love is the idea of being on the All-Star team."

"The operative word is *team*!" Annie reminded her. "Haven't you ever heard that old saying? 'There's no "I" in team'!"

"That's true," said Holly, wiping her sweaty forehead with the back of her arm, "but if you shuffle the letters around, there's definitely a 'me' in it!"

"Fine," snapped Annie. "There's another saying: 'Payback's a bitch'!"

"Do what you have to do," Holly challenged, then skated off, leaving Annie fuming.

Play began again and this time, Holly was the jammer.

Two can play this game, thought Annie. Usually when she was playing blocker, Annie put all of her energy into doing whatever it took to stop the opposing jammer from getting past. But when Holly and the opposing jammer, Sharmila, sped up to the pack in a race to be first through, Annie barely bothered to swing her bottom in Sharmila's direction. She didn't make contact, and even moved her body slightly to get in Holly's way. Quickly shifting aside, she allowed Sharmila to slip past and become lead jammer.

It was sabotage, but Annie was too angry to care. She realized that she was intentionally hurting her own team's chances of winning the scrimmage, but this was personal. This was about making Holly look bad.

By the time the scrimmage was over, Annie and Holly's team had lost by a whopping twenty-seven points. It felt terrible. Even seeing the furious look on Holly's face didn't give Annie as much satisfaction as she'd hoped.

Panting, Annie bent over and rested her hands on her knees. She made it look as though she were catching her breath but really she was averting her eyes from the other team's victory celebration. It was pretty obvious why they'd won − since Sharmila and Carmen weren't trying out for the All-Stars, they continued to play as they always had − with the best interests of their team at heart. But Annie and Holly had done the exact opposite.

If Annie had been more of a team player, maybe she and Holly would be the ones whooping it up right now.

Coach Ritter blew her whistle and motioned for the Belles to join her on the side of the track.

Annie could see the disappointment in Coach's eyes. "Do you girls think I was born yesterday?" she asked, shaking her head. "Did you think I wouldn't see what you were trying to do? Suddenly, everyone is trying to out-skate, out-block and out-jam everyone else in a misguided effort to make the All-Star squad. Well, ladies, that's not how it works!" She swept her gaze across the group, finally landing on Holly and Annie. "If you let your teammate down, you let yourself down. This isn't about showing off. All-Stars are team players, first and foremost. So I suggest you all start playing like the Belles I've come to know and respect. Got it?"

The girls nodded and muttered their apologies.

"One last thing before you leave," said Coach. "My old team, the Illinoisies, are going to be offering a training camp, or 'Roller Derby Boot Camp', for high school students over February break. I've left a pile of registration forms on the rental counter for anyone who might be interested in attending."

The girls waited until Coach Ritter had gone before storming the rental booth.

"Where is the camp being held?" Lauren asked Annie. "Here in Liberty Heights?"

"Um…" Annie scanned the paperwork. "Nope. It's going to take place at Great Lakes University."

"So it's a sleep-away camp?" Lauren said grimly. "That's about two hours away from here."

Holly let out a joyful shriek. "That is so cool! We'll get to live on campus, party in the dorms … and flirt with the college guys." Then she shrugged and added, "Oh. And skate of course."

Sharmila rolled her eyes and smiled. "Glad to see you've got your priorities in order, Holl." She picked up a registration booklet and began flipping through it.

"We can be roomies!" Holly cried, dropping an arm around Sharmila's shoulder.

But Sharmila shook her head and pointed to the dates printed on the form. "Not me," she said sadly. "The camp is the week of my grandparents' wedding anniversary. I need to help my parents with the party. The form says all campers have to stay on campus and take part for the entire week." She sighed and handed the form to Holly.

"I can't go either," said Lauren. "My grandparents will be here from Arizona that week. I haven't seen them in over a year, so I really don't want to miss their visit."

When some of the other Belles saw the cost of the camp, they knew it would be out of the question for them, too. And Liz and Carmen had already said they'd be opting out of derby activities for the spring, so they wouldn't make it either.

There was an uncomfortable silence as Annie realized that Holly was the only other player considering attending the camp.

Annie felt a wave of guilt for even wanting to go – money was tight so she couldn't very well ask her dad to fund the trip.

Mum, of course, was another story entirely. She earned a generous salary as a lawyer. Back in England, she'd gladly paid for Annie's elite gymnastics training, which was expensive. So maybe she'd be willing to pay Annie's boot camp tuition? Mum hadn't been overly keen on roller derby when Annie first started, but when she realized how much it meant to Annie, and seen her in action when she'd visited Liberty Heights, she'd had a change of heart. Asking her to foot the bill for the camp might be pushing things, but still, Annie could ask.

It was worth a shot.

"Hey…" Holly's voice jolted Annie out of her thoughts.

"Oh. Hey."

"Listen," said Holly. "I was a jerk out there."

"So was I," Annie admitted. "I'm sorry. Coach was right about teamwork."

"Yeah." Holly nodded. "So let's stop being losers and start acting like the champions we are. Friends?"

Annie smiled. "Friends!" she said, wrapping Holly in a hug. "And if I can manage to swing the camp cost, maybe you'd consider rooming with me?"

"I was going to ask you the same thing," Holly said, laughing. "I really do hope you'll be able to come. After all, we Belles have to stick together, right?"

"Right. On and off the track."

"Look out, college boys!" cried Holly.

Annie laughed but didn't comment. Personally, she had enough trouble trying to make sense of high school boys. If she was lucky enough to go to the boot camp, the last thing she would be worried about was flirting with college boys. She'd seen *Animal House* (one of Dad's favourite old movies) enough times to know how fraternity parties could turn out. No thanks!

As she followed the others to the lockers to change, she threw an arm around Lauren.

"So it looks like my derby wife and I will be taking separate holidays this February," she joked. "I hope our marriage

42

can survive it."

Surprisingly, Lauren didn't laugh at Annie's quip. Instead, her eyes went serious, as though she wanted to tell Annie something important.

"Is something wrong?" Annie asked gently.

Lauren hesitated, then shook her head. "Nah. I'm just disappointed about missing camp." She managed a small smile. "But you've got to promise me the minute you get back you'll teach me everything you learned."

"It's a deal." Annie laughed. "And, of course, since I'm rooming with Holly I'll probably get coaching in how to pick up guys! Don't worry – I'll pass on everything I learn."

"Yeah," said Lauren, forcing a smile and then glancing away. "Great."

Lauren didn't look very happy, and Annie didn't blame her. Boot camp sounded amazing and she'd be upset if she couldn't go either. Which was why she HAD to persuade her mum.

Chapter Five

"Why do they have to make turkey tacos?" Annie wondered, poking at the disgusting, vaguely Mexican gloop on her plate. "I know they're healthier, but it seems like such a cheat. Tacos should be beef. With lots of sour cream and spicy sauce."

"Well, the cafeteria isn't exactly known for its international cuisine," said Lauren, taking the seat across from Annie and opening her lunch bag.

Annie picked up one of the soggy shells. She brought it to her lips, but immediately put it down again. Not because the ground turkey smelled dodgy (which it did), but because what she spotted across the cafeteria was enough to turn her stomach.

Kelsey was sitting on Tyler's lap, and they were in the middle of a full-on make-out session.

Lexie, who was seated beside Annie, rolled her eyes. "Where do they think they are? The Honeymoon Suite at the Motel 6?"

Annie pushed her tray away with a sigh.

"Annie, please," said Lexie, biting into her veggie burger, "you've got to get over this. I don't mean to sound unsympathetic, but you are *so* better off without that cretin."

"I know, I know," groaned Annie. And she *did* know. She was fully aware that Tyler was a stuck-up idiot. It was just a major blow to her ego to see him lip-locked with someone else. And the fact that the someone else was Kelsey made it even worse.

"PDAs are in such bad taste," said Lauren disapprovingly.

"I know," Lexie agreed. "I've never been a fan of Public Displays of Affection. Although, given that we're talking about someone as toxic as Kelsey, maybe it's more like a Public Display of *In*fection."

Lauren giggled. "Ewww!"

Annie couldn't stop herself from sneaking another peek. Tyler had his hands in Kelsey's hair and she had her arms around his neck.

"He was such a good kisser," she said, sighing. The words were out before Annie could stop them. She felt her cheeks turn red when Lauren's eyes flew open.

"Well, I'm not surprised," said Lexie dryly. "I mean, clearly, he likes to practise."

Annie laughed in spite of her mood and helped herself to one of the barbeque-flavoured crisps on Lexie's tray.

"Seriously, though," said Lexie, patting Annie's shoulder.

"Love bites."

"I'll drink to that," said Annie. She lifted her can of Diet Coke in a toast and Lauren bumped her milk carton against it.

A burst of static from the PA system got everyone's attention. In the next moment, the principal's overly cheerful voice filled the cafeteria.

"It's that time of year again, students! Tickets for our annual Valentine's Day dance, the Cupid Cotillion, will go on sale tomorrow before homeroom. Love is in the air!"

"Ohhhh," said Lexie with a grin. "So *that's* what's in the air. And here I thought it was just the stench of turkey tacos."

"Happy bloody Valentine's Day," said Annie, taking a hefty gulp of Coke, then belching loudly.

Lexie and Lauren laughed.

"I can't believe they actually call it the Cupid Cotillion," sniggered Lexie. "The Stupid Cotillion would be more accurate."

"Forget about the dance and those two tongue wrestlers," Lauren advised, shooting another look in Tyler's direction. "You've got our anti-Valentine's Day bout to look forward to."

"That's ALL I've got to look forward to on Valentine's Day," said Annie glumly.

"Don't be so sure," said Lexie.

Annie frowned at her. "What are you talking about?"

"Jesse," said Lexie. "It's so obvious he's crazy about you. Maybe he'll be your valentine."

"Not this again," Annie said, laughing. "Lex, I've told you a zillion times, Jesse and I are just good friends. He's friendly with

46

all the roller girls."

"He sure spends an awful lot of time talking to you."

"Well, he talks to Lauren, too, and I don't see you making a fuss about them being more than friends." She turned to Lauren. "Right, Lauren? Just because you and Jesse chat now and then, that doesn't mean you want to hook up with him, does it?"

A strange little smile appeared on Lauren's face. "Not even a little bit."

"See?" Annie snatched another crisp from Lexie's tray and popped it into her mouth. "So enough about my love life, OK? Let's talk about you two. There has to be some boy you fancy, Lex. Spill!"

"Oh, I 'fancy' lots of boys," said Lexie. "Like Robert Pattinson and Trey Songz. Unfortunately, since they're not likely to show up at a high school Valentine's Day dance, I guess I'm out of luck."

"Really?" said Annie. "There's not a single boy in this school you might be interested in? Not even one?"

Lexie replied with an evasive shrug, which made Annie wonder if maybe she really did have a secret crush on someone. But she knew better than to press the issue. If Lexie liked a boy, she'd tell Annie when she was ready.

"How about you, Lauren?" Lexie asked, clearly wanting to turn the attention away from herself. "Any Liberty Heights High boys on your radar at the moment?"

"Not at the moment," Lauren answered in a serious tone, then lowered her eyes and added softly, "not ever, actually."

Annie was confused. "Huh?"

"Do you mean you like a boy from another school?" Lexie prompted, then grinned. "Or maybe you're holding out for one of the One Direction guys?"

"Uh … not exactly." Lauren drew in a deep breath and looked up from the sandwich she'd been studying so intently. "The thing is, I'm not really interested in any guys. Famous or otherwise."

Annie couldn't help herself − she let out a tiny gasp. Not because she was horrified, but just because Lauren's revelation came as a surprise to her. Lauren, to her credit, did not drop her eyes back to her sandwich. She held her head high, meeting Annie and Lexie's gazes. Annie felt a rush of pride for her friend. Even in this day and age, coming out was a huge step.

Instinctively, Annie reached over and placed her hand on top of Lauren's. There was a tear in the corner of Lauren's eye.

"Wow. It feels really good to say that out loud," she said, her voice trembling slightly. "You guys are the first people I've told."

"Thank you for trusting us," Annie said softly. "That means a lot to me."

"Me, too." Lexie gave Lauren a warm smile. "Seriously … everyone should be proud of who they are. No apologies."

"Right," said Lauren, taking another steadying breath. "I mean, I know in my head and in my heart that there's nothing wrong with being gay. It's just a little scary to admit to being different. Especially around here, where everyone puts such a premium on being mainstream."

"Tell me about it," Lexie chuckled. "Being biracial, I've

48

kind of held the monopoly on 'different' around here. And believe me, I've taken my share of hits. But I've always thought mainstream was just another word for average. And who wants to be average?"

Annie thought back to her first few weeks in America, when everyone seemed so hung up on the fact that she spoke with an accent. It had become tedious to know that people only thought of her as "the English girl". Being considered different – even in that small way – had left her feeling frustrated and alone. And later, when she'd chosen to be a roller girl instead of a cheerleader, she'd learned what it was like to go against expectation. She could only imagine what it would be for her friend when people began to think of her as "the gay girl".

"Look," said Lauren. "I know being homosexual doesn't make me unique or special, or important, any more than you being heterosexual makes you unique or special. It's biology; it's DNA. You can't, like, take credit for it. In fact, it kind of bugs me when gay kids come out and then get all haughty about it, acting like their sexual preference is some kind of an accomplishment."

"No," said Annie. "It's not an accomplishment. But having the courage to face up to small-minded people who are going to judge you for it totally is."

And people would judge Lauren, Annie knew. They shouldn't, but they would. God! How incredibly ridiculous was that? It was like judging someone for being allergic to peanuts, or having brown eyes.

"Maybe those gay kids act like that because it's the only

way they can think of to shut small-minded people up," Lexie suggested.

Lauren considered this. "Could be," she allowed, then chuckled. "Wow. I'm a gay teen and even *I'm* judging gay teens."

Annie smiled. "Don't be so hard on yourself. This is complicated stuff. Just being a teenager at all is challenging enough."

"So you're really OK with this?" There was still a tiny thread of worry in Lauren's voice. "I mean, this doesn't change anything about our friendship, does it?"

Annie shook her head emphatically. "Absolutely not!" She laughed. "You're still my derby wife. And even when you get a girlfriend, that's not going to change. She'll just have to understand that we're a package deal."

"Thanks." Lauren looked visibly relieved. "Actually one of the reasons I'm not going to the derby boot camp is that I'm planning to come out to my whole family while my grandparents are visiting. I want everyone to find out together. I think they'll be shocked at first, but I'm pretty sure they'll be cool with it." She smiled. "If nothing else, at least it will get my mother's mind off my weight issues for a change!"

"By the way," said Lexie, "one of my favourite artists, Frida Kahlo, was bisexual." She laughed, looking slightly embarrassed. "I'm not sure what that has to do with anything. I guess it's just my way of saying you've got my support."

"Mine too," Annie assured Lauren. "And you always will."

Chapter Six

After school, Annie and Lexie headed straight to Rosie Lee's. Today was the day the Queen of Hearts advertisement was to appear in the *Liberty Heights Gazette* and Lexie couldn't wait to see her photographic work in print.

Annie was slightly less eager. She had no idea which of the photos was going to be featured in the ad; Dad had made the decision in secret. He promised Annie he'd pick the one he thought was the most eye-catching.

"What do you think about what Lauren told us at lunch?" Annie asked. "Were you as surprised as I was?"

"To tell you the truth," said Lexie, "not really. I mean, it's not like I always suspected it, because I never really thought about it one way or the other. But once she told us, I was like, oh, yeah.

That totally makes sense."

"It took guts," said Annie. "She could have just kept it quiet until college. I think she's pretty courageous coming out in high school."

"Me too," said Lexie. "I just hope some of the narrow-minded Neanderthals around here don't give her too hard a time about it."

When they entered the café, Dad hustled out from behind the counter, waving a copy of the *Gazette* in the air. The handful of customers who were sipping their afternoon tea looked up to see what all the excitement was about.

"It's here!" he cried, meeting the girls in the middle of the shop.

"How does it look?" asked Annie, nervously biting her lower lip. "Which one did you use? Please tell me you picked a good shot."

"They were all good shots," said Dad, grinning at Lexie. "But I haven't seen it in print yet, because I've been waiting for you two to get here so we could all admire it together."

"So what are we waiting for?" cried Lexie. "Let's check it out."

Annie took the paper and flipped through it. She found the advert four pages in, next to the horoscopes and the local cinema listings.

It was the shot in which her father was holding the tray out to offer her a tart and she was daintily reaching for one. She was smiling, and the dress really did show off her figure.

Unfortunately, there was no getting away from the puffy sleeves and the crown. But all in all, it could have been much worse.

"It's awesome!" said Lexie, beaming. "I love this one. You both look awesome."

"I guess I don't look like a complete idiot," Annie conceded. "Maybe only slightly dorky."

"Nothing dorky about it," Dad declared. "You look positively regal. And once the good subjects of your kingdom have had a chance to read their afternoon papers, I bet we'll be flooded with orders for Valentine's goodies."

"Well, then I guess that means I should get to work," said Annie, slipping her backpack off her shoulders and taking an apron off the peg rack.

"I'm gonna stick around for a cup of coffee," said Lexie, who worshipped three things in life: art, individuality, and good coffee. "Then I'll have to head home and get started on my homework."

"Help yourself," said Dad, motioning to the coffee machine behind the counter. "After all, you're practically one of the staff."

Lexie giggled and poured herself a steaming cup of French roast, while Annie tied on an apron.

While Annie set about brewing a fresh pot of hazelnut decaf, Dad took a few minutes to show the advertisement to the customers in the shop, who all agreed that it really captured the fun spirit of Rosie Lee's. When he finally joined Annie behind the counter, it suddenly occurred to her that she still hadn't got around to mentioning the boot camp to him.

"Um, Dad?"

"Yes, Beanie?" Dad had teased Annie with the nickname String Bean, or Beanie for short, ever since the growth spurt that had meant she'd had to give up gymnastics.

"There's something I'd like to run by you."

"OK," said Dad, smiling. "But if it's about swapping cranberries for golden raisins in the scone recipe, I'm way ahead of you."

Annie grinned. "No, Dad. It's not about raisins. It's about … boot camp."

"Boot camp?" Dad gave her an incredulous look. "As in army boot camp?"

"As in roller derby boot camp," said Annie, giggling. "I'm pretty sure the US army doesn't enlist fourteen-year-olds. But Great Lakes University is hosting a week-long boot camp for roller girls. And, um, well, I'd really like to go. If that's OK."

Dad studied her for a moment, then abruptly squared his shoulders and lifted his chin. "So, you want go to roller derby boot camp, Private?" he barked, taking on the attitude of an army drill sergeant. "Can you handle it, soldier? Do you have what it takes?"

"Well, I'm not sure," said Annie with a hopeful look. "Because, what it takes … is six hundred dollars."

"Did you say six hundred dollars?"

"Sir!" Annie snapped him a salute. "Sir, yes, Sir!"

"Wow." Dad's shoulders slumped. "I think you just lost the battle, soldier."

"Wait," said Annie. "You haven't heard me out. Coach is

putting together an All-Star squad and going to this camp will really help my chances of getting chosen for the team. I can probably pay part of the cost with what I've earned working here ... but, well, I was thinking I'd ask Mum for the rest of the money." Annie realized she was wringing her hands. She took a deep breath and asked: "Would you mind if I approached her about it?"

Dad's eyebrows were knitted together. Annie knew he was thinking about the little thrill of triumph his soon-to-be ex-wife would get out of being able to help pay for something he couldn't afford. Suddenly, Annie felt like a traitor.

"Never mind, Dad," she said quickly. "I should never have mentioned it. Really. It's no big deal. I can go next year."

"Annie—"

"Honestly. Mum's still not thrilled about me playing roller derby."

She picked up a towel and began wiping the condensation from the inside of the display case. As much as she wanted to go to this camp, she refused to allow Dad to feel inferior to Mum.

She'd just have to work on her derby skills on her own. For free.

Dad sighed and pulled Annie into a big hug. "You're amazing, you know that, Beanie? The best. You don't have to feel guilty about going to Mum for something I can't give you. She's your parent just as much as I am."

"I just don't want her to think that our shop is a failure," Annie said.

Dad smiled. "Just the fact that you called it 'our' shop means more to me than you can even imagine. That alone is worth the six hundred bucks."

Annie knew exactly what he meant. When Dad had begun talking about the shop her mother had called it "David's folly". But since the very first day they'd entered the rundown old diner to sweep out the cobwebs and grime, Rosie Lee's had been close to Annie's heart, too. Even her hard-to-impress mother had fallen for Rosie Lee's charm when she came to visit back in November.

"It is *our* shop," she assured her father, feeling a lump in her throat. "We're in this together. You may be the official owner and head baker, but I'm Vice President of Icing and Chief Executive of Coffee Brewing!"

Dad laughed. "That's quite a title. I think you may be due for a pay rise."

"And don't forget me," said Lexie, raising her hand. "Practically one of the staff, remember?"

"Right," said Dad, nodding at the mural on the wall. Lexie had painted a red London double-decker bus, whose passengers were famous characters from British history and literature. "You're our Creative Director, not to mention our one-woman advertising department." He smiled and gave Annie another hug. "You go ahead and negotiate with Mum for the financial backing. If she says yes, it's fine with me."

Annie was about to jump for joy, when she remembered. "There's one other problem."

"What's that?"

"I'll be gone for a whole week. And it's the week the school's on holiday so you'll probably get tons of customers, especially with the advert running. If I go away, you'll have no one to help you in the shop."

"Um, *hell-oh?*" drawled Lexie, rolling her eyes. "What part of '*practically one of the staff*' do you guys not understand?"

Both Annie and her dad turned to stare at Lexie.

"*You* want to fill in for me while I'm at camp?" Annie didn't even try to hide the disbelief in her voice.

"Sure," said Lexie. "Why wouldn't I? I mean, I hang around here enough. I know how everything works, I've got the menu memorized—"

"True," said Dad, warily. "It's just that, well … I don't really see you as the 'customer service' type."

Lexie laughed. "You don't have to tiptoe around it. I know I can be somewhat … um, *caustic* at times. But I promise I'll be an absolute angel the whole time I'm working here. Efficient, charming, and courteous." She gave them an exaggerated wink. "And if I happen to spill boiling coffee on some obnoxious customer, I promise I'll make it look like an accident."

Dad gulped and whispered to Annie, "She's kidding, right?"

"Of course she's kidding, Dad. Lexie would never spill coffee on a customer," Annie giggled. "That would be a waste of perfectly good coffee!"

"Seriously, Mr Turner," said Lexie, "I'd love to work here while Annie's away. I'm saving up for a new graphics tablet and I need to pull in some cash."

"See? That proves she'll be nice to the customers," teased Annie. "She needs the tips!"

"Well then," said Dad, as the door jingled to announce a new customer's arrival, "it looks like the VP of Icing might be heading to camp!"

Annie squealed with delight, gave him a kiss, then grabbed a menu to bring to the new customer. She could barely contain her excitement as she took down his order.

She was going to boot camp!

All she had to do now was convince Mum!

Chapter Seven

Annie had set her alarm for the crack of dawn on Friday morning. She rolled out of bed, made a groggy effort to smooth her long hair, then went over to her computer.

Moments later, the sound of the Skype signal filled her room, and seconds after that her mother's face appeared on the laptop's screen.

"Good morning, love," said Mum from behind the desk in her office. "You're up early!"

"I know," said Annie, smiling. "I wanted to be the first to wish you a happy Valentine's Day!"

"Oh…" Mum looked oddly flustered. "Well, thank you." Behind her glasses, Mum's pretty blue eyes darted to the corner of her desk where an enormous bouquet of roses stood.

"Wow." Annie raised her eyebrows, properly shocked. "Looks like somebody beat me to it."

Mum blushed. "Yes, actually."

This was just too weird. Mum receiving flowers on Valentine's Day from someone who wasn't Dad?

"Did Gran and Grandad send those?" Annie asked, picturing a card that read "Happy Valentine's Day to Our Darling Daughter". But even as she posed the question she knew what the answer would be.

"No, sweetheart." Mum forced a laugh. "You know Grandad. He always sends me chocolates."

For some reason, Annie couldn't even muster up a chuckle. Instead, she changed the subject.

"So, Mum, I um … I … well…" She sighed and decided to just cut to the chase. "I need some money, Mum."

Mum raised an eyebrow. "May I ask what it's for?"

Here we go…

"Camp," Annie replied, cagily.

"What sort of camp?"

"Well, roller derby camp, actually. At Great Lakes University."

Mum's mouth turned down slightly. "Of course. Roller derby."

Annie bristled, but refused to let this snowball into an argument. She took a steadying breath and willed herself to remain calm and reasonable. "I know you're still not completely on board with me playing derby, Mum. But think of all the other benefits that can come from me going to camp." Since Annie had anticipated her mother's reluctance, she'd prepared a little sales pitch last night. "First of all, I'll be away from home, on my own, for a whole week. The camp has plenty of supervision, of course, but this will be a great opportunity for me to start learning to be independent."

Mum sighed, but Annie noticed that she'd begun tapping her pencil on the desk, always a sign that she was considering something carefully. Annie barrelled on.

"And I'll be applying for college really, really soon. Well, OK, in a few years, but still, there's no point in waiting until the last minute to start thinking about where I'd like to go. And since the camp is being held at Great Lakes University, it could almost count as a college visit. I'll get an idea of how I feel about a big university campus."

Mum actually nodded at that and Annie smiled. She'd known that bringing up the whole "higher education" thing would definitely work in her favour. Mum was all about education.

"And most importantly," she said, gliding into her conclusion, "I know that one of the things you hate about derby is the fact that you think it's dangerous."

"It *is* dangerous…"

"OK, fine, it is a *little* dangerous, but this camp is going to be a great way for me to improve my skills. The more training I get, the less likely it is that I'll get hurt."

"…*Again*," her mother added pointedly, referring to Annie's ankle sprain a few months ago. "The less likely you'll be to get hurt *again*."

"Right," said Annie. Then she smiled, looked straight at the bouquet of roses and said, "I know camp tuition isn't as romantic as a dozen *roses*, but maybe you could consider it my Valentine's Day present?"

Again, Mum blushed.

Annie knew that last bit had been manipulative – but all's fair in love and derby. It was clear that Mum felt self-conscious about having an admirer. Hopefully she'd give Annie what she'd asked for as a way to soften the blow of finding out that her mother was dating.

Cheap shot, Annie knew. But she *really* wanted to go to boot camp.

Mum was quiet for a bit. Then, to Annie's surprise, she gave her a broad grin. "OK," she said, then held up her hand quickly before Annie could start shrieking for joy. "But it's not because I'm suddenly delighted about you playing roller derby." She narrowed her eyes playfully. "I'm not even giving it to you because you played the 'I'm the child of a broken home and now my mummy's dating' card."

It was Annie's turn to blush. "Oh. You picked up on that, did you?"

"Of course I did, you cheeky little thing!" Mum laughed. "I didn't get to where I am in my career by being easily manipulated."

Annie rolled her eyes and giggled. "OK. So why *are* you giving me the money?"

"Because," said her mother with a grin, "you gave one hell of a closing argument! That was pure Philippa Bradley DNA at work. I love knowing that you've got at least a little bit of me in you."

"I have a lot of you in me, Mum," said Annie sincerely.

Mum smiled. "You have no idea how glad I am to hear it," she said. "Now, then, just ask the camp to send me the bill."

They spent a few minutes talking about school, and the Valentine's specials Dad would be serving at Rosie Lee's.

"So," Annie said, wagging her eyebrows. "Who sent the flowers?"

Mum reached over to gently touch one of the beautiful red blooms. They were from a new colleague, a man a few years older than Mum, whose wife had passed away a couple of years ago. The flowers had arrived that morning with a note inviting her to dinner.

"I'm happy for you, Mum," Annie said, then winked. "Just don't do anything I wouldn't!"

This time Mum's cheeks turned as red as the roses. "Annie Turner!" she sputtered, giggling. "You're terrible."

Annie laughed. It was kind of weird talking to her mum about dating. But she was truly pleased for her. It wasn't just nice for Mum, it also took the edge off Annie's guilt over leaving her mother alone in London.

"I'm glad you have a date," Annie said. Then, after she'd signed off from Skype, she added under her breath, "At least one of us does."

* * *

"Heart-shaped pancakes!" Dad announced when Annie appeared in the kitchen. "The official breakfast food of Valentine's Day!"

"Yum," said Annie, taking a seat, her mouth watering at the delicious smell of buttery pancakes and raspberry sauce. "Hey, remember that time you tried mixing Love Hearts into the batter?" she asked, giggling.

Dad winced. "Not one of my better attempts," he admitted. "Really chalky and far too crunchy."

"Not to mention the pancakes came out a sickly grey colour!" Annie reminded him.

"I was merely a novice chef at the time. I've improved since then."

"No question!" said Annie, biting into a warm pancake dripping with red sauce.

"Be right back," said Dad, turning off the griddle. "I'm going out to get the newspaper."

Annie went on enjoying her breakfast until Dad returned to slide a bright pink envelope across the table towards her. "ANNIE" was written in neat cursive letters across the front.

"Oh, Dad," said Annie, feeling bad that she hadn't thought to get her father a card, "you didn't have to."

"I didn't," said Dad. "It was in the mailbox with the newspaper."

Annie laughed. "Sure it was."

"No, really," said Dad, with a guilty look. "I've been so busy at the shop I never got around to hitting the card store. Sorry."

"No need to apologize," said Annie, taking the last bite of her delicious breakfast. "Besides, who needs Valentine's cards when you've got Valentine's *carbs*?"

"True." Dad laughed. "But that doesn't solve the mystery of who sent this one."

Annie eyed the handwriting. It didn't look familiar, but if she had to bet, her money was on Lexie. In fact, it was probably a custom-designed, hand-drawn card. Annie would save it and someday, when her best friend was a famous artist, it would be worth millions. She sighed, wishing she'd got a card for Lexie.

As Dad set about cleaning up the pancake mess, Annie opened the envelope.

But to her surprise, it did not contain a Lexie Jones original, or even a store-bought greetings card. It was a CD.

"What've you got there?" Dad asked from the sink.

"Oh, it's something called a compact disc," Annie teased. "It's the great-grandchild of the cassette tape. Third cousin twice removed of the vinyl record."

"Ha ha," Dad dead-panned. "I meant who is it from?"

Annie peered into the envelope but there was no card, just the CD. She turned it over and saw that it had been inscribed on the front. In the same steady handwriting that appeared on the envelope it read:

HAPPY VALENTINE'S DAY, ANNIE. YOU ROCK!

No signature.

Now Annie was beginning to understand.

"Well?" Dad prompted.

"Gee, I don't know," said Annie with wide eyes and a tone of exaggerated puzzlement. "I guess it must be from a secret admirer."

"Yes," said Dad with a straight face. "I guess it is."

"Dad!" Annie smiled. "Come on. I know this is from you! What did you do? Download a bunch of songs I used to like when I was little or something?"

"I plead innocent," said Dad throwing up his hands in surrender. "Honest."

"Right," said Annie. "I'm guessing it's *The Best of the Teletubbies*. Or maybe *Mopatop Shop's Greatest Hits*."

"Really, Annie…" Dad shook his head. "It wasn't me. For one thing, I would never bring those Teletubbies back into our lives because they used to drive me crazy. And for another thing…" He trailed off, grinning.

"What? What other thing?"

"Annie, you're a beautiful young lady. Do really think the only possible explanation for a mysterious valentine is that your old man sent it?"

"Wait…" Annie frowned. Truly, she hadn't even thought the CD could be from anyone else. "You think it's from, like … a *boy*? Like, some kind of secret admirer?"

Dad rolled his eyes. "*Like* … duh."

"That's ridiculous!"

"Is it?" Dad was smiling from ear to ear.

Could it really be? Annie felt a tiny tingle of excitement in her belly. Was it even possible? Maybe Tyler had come to his senses and this was his way of getting her back.

No. She was being delusional now. After that public hook-up with Kelsey in the cafeteria, Annie knew there was no way Tyler was going to come grovelling back to her.

So Dad was just pulling her leg. That was the only rational conclusion.

"Someone's crushing on Annnn-ie," Dad sang in a silly voice. "Someone's crushing on—"

Annie sighed, pushing away from the table and leaving the kitchen. She knew Dad was just trying to have a little fun with her, and that he hadn't meant any harm, but for a minute, all his talk about a secret admirer had got her hopes up.

She ran upstairs to grab her school things and tossed the CD unceremoniously on her desk.

Even if Dad's attempts at Valentine's Day humour were well-intentioned, she just wasn't in the mood for jokes.

Because the truth of the matter was that *no one* was crushing on Annie.

Annie was feeling better by the time she got to school. Despite the fact that she didn't have a Valentine's date, she did have something just as good to look forward to: boot camp.

She also had a backpack full of heart-shaped cookies iced with pink and red swirls. Dad had baked them especially for her to hand out to her friends at school. She suspected he didn't mind the fact that samples of his delicious baked goods circulating around Liberty Heights High also qualified as advertising for Rosie Lee's, but Annie had no problem with that.

But as she walked the corridors towards her locker, she began to notice that people were giving her strange looks.

Maybe they could smell the freshly baked cookies she had with her?

Or maybe the fact that she'd worn a red sweater and tied her ponytail in a pink ribbon made her look silly and babyish?

But, no, that couldn't be it. Plenty of the girls – even the cool ones – were decked out in Valentine's-Day-themed outfits.

So why was everyone staring?

Annie received the very unpleasant answer the minute she reached her locker. A wave of humiliation crashed over her when she saw what was taped to the front: the Queen of Hearts advert from the *Gazette*, with Annie in her cartoonish gown and crown.

That alone would have been bad enough, but there was more.

Whoever had posted the advert on her locker had written the word "SKANK", in big, red block letters right across Annie's image.

Skank? she thought. *Me?*

Her mind whirled back to a time when she'd heard some girls referring to roller girls as "sluts on wheels". That remark had been infuriating, but this insult seemed so much worse somehow, because this one was directed solely at Annie.

This one was personal.

She was vaguely aware that a small crowd had gathered around her, but all she could do was stand mutely, staring at her ruined photo.

Suddenly Lexie was there, pushing through the onlookers and tearing the picture down from the locker. She crumpled it fiercely and said, loud enough for everyone to hear: "Obviously *somebody* is jealous!" She put her arm around Annie and began to lead her away from the crowd. "And that's because *somebody* knows she's just a rebound!"

And just as she and Lexie ducked into the bathroom, Annie caught a glimpse of Kelsey strolling down the hallway, her arm around Tyler's waist. On her pretty face was a smug, vindictive look, a look that confirmed all of Annie's suspicions. She didn't need a handwriting sample to know that Kelsey had written the nasty word that kept running through Annie's head.

Skank.

Chapter Eight

Annie went through the day in a daze, numbed by a strange mixture of embarrassment, hurt, and anger. Time and again, she had to push the image of the defaced photo out of her mind.

By the end of the day, all she wanted to do was go home, climb into bed, and pull the covers over her head. She confided as much in Lauren, who frowned.

"You're not going to let that sneaky, stuck-up little cheerleader make you miss the anti-Valentine's Day bout, are you?"

Annie's eyes flew open. "The bout! Oh my god, I was so preoccupied with Kelsey's prank, I forgot all about it." She smiled for the first time since arriving at her locker that morning. "If there's one thing I could do with right now, it's a night of derby action!"

Just the thought of skating with her team breathed new life into Annie. She'd channel her anger into energy. If she went out there and imagined that every single one of her opponents was actually Kelsey, the Belles would thrash the High Rollers for sure!

As Dad's ancient truck chugged and whined through the streets of Liberty Heights, there were more than a few moments when Annie thought the poor pickup might give up all together. By some miracle, though, they made it to the rink without incident.

As they pushed through the glass doors, Annie thought Dad seemed a little nervous. She was about to ask him what was on his mind when she remembered that Jesse had asked Dad to be the bout commentator tonight. It would be the first time her father would be announcing the entire game over the loudspeaker.

Stage fright, she thought. *Poor Dad.*

But any pity she was feeling evaporated the moment her dad marched directly up to Coach Ritter. Annie watched from a distance as her coach and her father shared an extremely warm smile. Only then did she notice he was holding a small plastic container which he presented with a chivalrous flourish to a beaming Coach Ritter. Inside the box sat a pink cupcake with creamy white frosting. Perched atop the frosting was an elegant chocolate heart.

Annie was gobsmacked! She knew every item on Rosie

Lee's Valentine's menu and pretty little pink cupcakes were definitely *not* among them. As far as she could tell the perfect little confection was a one-off − baked by her father especially for Coach Ritter.

Woah. Romantic.

Coach was looking at the cupcake with shining eyes − she looked so happy it may as well have been a diamond ring! Then Coach leaned forward and placed a lingering kiss on Dad's cheek.

Annie felt a weird tumble in her stomach. It wasn't that she was grossed out exactly, it was just a little strange to think that her dad was dating. The part that *was* a little hard to swallow, however, was the fact that it was Valentine's Day and, while both her parents had new love interests, Annie was without a single romantic prospect.

"Well they look cosy."

Annie whirled to find Jesse smiling at her. She shook her head, still feeling a bit waylaid by what she'd just witnessed. "Huh?"

"Your dad and Coach Ritter." Jesse motioned with his head in their direction. "Personally, I think they make a great couple."

"Oh. Right. Yeah." Annie smiled. "I agree, actually. It's very romantic."

"So you're embracing the whole Cupid's arrow vibe, then?"

"For them, yes," said Annie. "For me? No way."

Jesse looked confused, and strangely disappointed. "You're not having a good Valentine's Day?"

"Not exactly," said Annie. "I'll recap it for you. First, at breakfast, I get an anonymous CD disguised as a valentine from a – " she jerked her fingers to mime a pair of air quotes – "*secret admirer.*"

"And that's a bad thing?" Jesse asked, frowning.

"Well, it wouldn't have been except that the so-called secret admirer was actually my Dad."

"Uh…" Jesse blinked. "Are you sure about that?"

"Without a shadow of a doubt – it's exactly the sort of silly joke he loves. I mean, who else would send me an anonymous gift?"

"No idea." Jesse gave a casual shrug, but his face looked a little strained. "But, um, did you even play it?"

"Play what?" asked Annie, suddenly preoccupied as she noticed that he was wearing his black-and-white-striped official's jersey – it was a hideous polyester thing, but somehow, Jesse managed to make it look cool. In fact, he rocked it. Maybe it had something to do with his tousled mop of black hair. Or his torn and faded blue jeans.

"Annie … did you hear what I just said?"

"Huh?" Annie snapped her gaze up from the jersey to look at his face. "What?"

"I asked you if you played it. The CD. Ya know, I was just thinking that maybe the songs on it would give you a clue as to who sent it."

"I'm telling you I didn't *have* to play it," Annie sighed, feeling exasperated. "Because I knew who it was from."

"Your dad."

"Yes!" Annie nodded vigorously. "Jesse, do you want to know

the problem with Valentine's Day?"

Jesse cocked an eyebrow. "There's a problem with it?"

"Oh, yes. A big one. See, the thing is, Valentine's Day is absolutely lovely if you're with someone. The problem is if you *don't* have a significant other – that's such a stupid term, isn't it? Anyway, if you don't happen to have one of those, then Valentine's Day is just a big fat reminder of how completely and utterly *alone* you are. It's as though all the florists and greetings card companies and chocolate manufacturers in the whole wide world are pointing at you and laughing their heads off. And while they're raking in all their Valentine's Day profits, people like you and me—"

"You and me?"

"Yes, you and me. Me and you."

Jesse grinned. "Just makin' sure I heard you right."

"People like you and me who *aren't* buying or receiving flowers and cards are simply left to feel forgotten and unloved!"

Jesse scratched his chin thoughtfully. "Did I say I felt unloved?"

"Well, no…"Annie shrugged. "I just assumed."

"Oh."

"Don't you? Feel unloved, I mean."

"Well, I *didn't*," Jesse admitted with another crooked grin. "But after hearing this little tirade of yours, I'm thinking maybe I should."

"Oh, Jess. I'm sorry." Annie reached over and touched his arm. "I didn't mean to get you down."

"Ah…" Jesse chuckled. "Don't worry about it. I'll bounce back.

Meanwhile, I'd better get over to the sound system. Carmen's little brother Roberto is filling in as DJ while I ref. I burned an awesome anti-Valentine's-Day CD for tonight's soundtrack."

Annie smiled at last, the thought of cool music helping her to shake off her sulky mood. "I hope you included 'Kiss Off', by the Violent Femmes?"

"Of course."

"Good. How about Joy Division's 'Love Will Tear Us Apart'?"

Jesse nodded.

"And 'Sgt. Pepper's Lonely Hearts Club Band'?"

"Are you kidding? It's practically the anti-Valentine's-Day anthem."

Annie laughed, which felt surprisingly good after her angry rant.

"I'm impressed that you got 'em all," said Jesse. "You rock."

"Ha! You're not the only one who thinks so," said Annie. "That's exactly what my Dad wrote on my Valentine's CD. Great minds think alike, eh? By the way, you rock too."

"Thanks. Sooo … you gonna be all right?" Jesse asked.

"Yeah, I'm fine." Annie motioned towards the lockers and smiled. "In the immortal words of Billy Shears, 'I'll get by with a little help from my friends.'"

"Good." Jesse turned to leave, but swung back, blue eyes twinkling. "And for what it's worth … don't write off secret admirers completely. They just might surprise you."

With that, he turned again and hurried across the rink to meet up with Roberto. Annie watched him go, feeling confused by his last comment. Then Liz was calling to her from the locker room doorway to come and join the others. It was almost time for the bout to begin. And there was nothing like a bad day to bring out the competitive spirit of a roller girl.

Annie, or rather Anne R. Key, was more ready than she'd ever been to kick some serious butt!

Dad's voice boomed through the rink. "Good evening, all you lonely hearts!" he said. "It's Valentine's Day, folks, and that means tonight it's all about love. Do you know what I love? Roller derby!"

The crowd roared as the Liberty Belles and the High Rollers took to the track, introduced by Dad. Both teams had gone all out in the wardrobe department. Everyone was sporting some shade of red or pink but they'd put a "down with love" spin on things. Tessa Distressa from the High Rollers was wearing a red T-shirt with shiny black lips printed on the front. On the back of her hot-pink booty shorts she'd painted the words: "CUPID CAN KISS MY ASS!"

Roberto hit the play button and J. Giels Band's "Love Stinks" blared out.

"Right, Annie, you'll start as jammer," announced Coach Ritter.

Yes! thought Annie, *finally something good's happening today.* But her heart sank when she noticed that Dee Stroyer was her opposing jammer.

The bout began and the fans cheered the girls as they buzzed around the track. In an effort to psyche Annie out, Dee Stroyer skated up close to her and actually snarled.

Nice try, thought Annie. But after the day she'd just endured, it was going to take a lot more than a dirty look to throw her. She reminded herself that Dee was the reason her cool outfit of red shorts and a pink T-shirt with a heart split down the middle was marred by the ugly brace she still had to wear on her left ankle. Then for good measure, she summoned an image of Kelsey smirking as she strutted along on Tyler's arm. These two visuals were all the inspiration Annie needed.

Annie shifted her weight and leaned low, expertly accelerating and cutting in front of Dee Stroyer with no warning whatsoever. Pushing through the pack, Annie become lead jammer. After scoring four points, she quickly called off the jam. When she looked back at her opponent, she was pleased to see that she'd wiped the cocky snarl off Dee Stroyer's face!

Fuelled by Jesse's clever anti-romance soundtrack, the Belles took an early lead and maintained it throughout the match.

Annie was having an exceptional night. She was playing aggressively, but only had one brief stint in the sin bin. On her next outing as jammer, Annie scored eight points. *I'm not a* SKANK, Annie mused silently, after barrelling through the pack and scoring four more points. *I'm a* TANK!

The hostility that had surfaced at the Belle's last practice was gone entirely. They were playing like the league champions they were, completely in tune with one another. Annie helped Holly score by whipping her ahead of the pack, and when Annie was jammer, Holly returned the favour by bootie-blocking a High Rollers blocker so that Annie could bomb past her and score.

The bout ended in a decisive 180 to 127 victory to the Belles.

"Let's show some love for ALL these roller girls who won our hearts tonight," said Dad over the microphone, as the crowd erupted in cheers.

As the Belles celebrated with fist bumps and high fives, Annie sought out Holly, catching her in a bear hug.

"Nice work out there, *roomie!*" she cried.

It took Holly only a second to understand. "You're coming to boot camp!" Holly beamed. "We're gonna be room-mates!"

Annie shook hands with some of the High Rollers, but Dee Stroyer pretended that she didn't see Annie's outstretched hand.

What a sore loser! thought Annie, hoping that Coach Ritter had clocked Dee's poor sportsmanship.

Dad was waiting at the side of the track to congratulate her with a hug and a kiss.

"You sure you need to go to that boot camp?" he teased.

"There's always more to learn," Annie assured him. "Hey, Dad, do you mind if I go to the Sugar Shack for ice cream with some of the girls?"

"Not at all," said Dad. "As long as you don't mind if go out for dinner with Coach Ritter."

Annie was impressed. "You asked her out?"

"Actually," said Dad with a wink, "she asked me out."

"Wow!" Annie couldn't suppress the slight twinge of envy she felt over the fact that her father was going on a Valentine's date while she was single. Still, she was happy for him. And for Coach, too. Returning the wink, she gave him the same advice she'd given Mum: "Don't do anything I wouldn't."

In the locker room the girls hurried out of their derby clothes quickly in order to get to the ice cream parlour before it closed.

"Just a warning," said Lauren, "but if I see some starry-eyed couple sharing an ice cream sundae, I seriously might throw up."

"Oh, I wouldn't worry about that," said Annie, laughing. "After all, there's nothing like a bunch of sweaty roller girls sitting at the next table to kill a romantic mood."

"Wish I could join you," said Holly, grinning. "But I just got a text from a hot guy in my Math class. He asked me to meet him at a party."

Annie rolled her eyes and pretended to be miffed. "Haven't you ever heard the 'Never Ditch Your Friends for a Guy', rule?"

"Yes, and I abide by that law three hundred and sixty-four days a year. But on Valentine's Day, there's a loophole."

Annie laughed. "Have fun, roomie."

As the group headed towards the rink exit, Annie spotted Jesse disconnecting his iPod from the sound system. She marched over to him, smiling broadly.

"Hey, Jess, wanna go to the Sugar Shack for a sundae?"

Jesse's whole face seemed to light up at the invitation. He looked ready to accept then he noticed the rest of the girls waiting by the door.

"You're all going?" he asked.

Annie laughed. "Yeah. We're taking a stand against the commonly held belief that you can only enjoy Valentine's Day in pairs."

Jesse gave her a strange look, then shook his head. "Thanks, but I think I'll pass," he said, then disappeared behind the rental booth to grab his coat.

The girls were a little disappointed that Jesse had opted out. As they continued to the exit, Annie was about to propose that someone should go after him and talk him into changing his mind.

But before she could suggest it, Carmen giggled. "Of course he doesn't want to come with us," she said in a knowing tone. "It's Valentine's Day. A hottie like Jesse is bound to have a major date lined up."

Annie stopped dead in her tracks.

Jesse. On a date. The thought had never even crossed her mind. She'd just *assumed* he was single, but she'd never actually asked him.

She followed the others out to the parking lot, where the girls divided themselves between Liz's car and Carmen's, which was actually her mother's minivan. Annie tried to imagine who Jesse might be taking out. No one jumped immediately to mind. There was that redheaded junior girl she'd seen him talking to in the library last week. And hadn't he mentioned a girl named Kiki (or was it Koko?) from the skateboard park once or twice? Annie seemed to recall that she'd asked him to help her replace the grip tape on her skateboard deck, but that didn't sound like a hot and heavy romance.

Well, it really didn't matter, did it? Maybe Jesse *was* dating the library girl. Or maybe little Miss Halfpipe Rider was rocking Jesse's world with her gnarly nose grinds and ollies.

Maybe he *was* going on a Valentine's date. Whatever. It really didn't matter to Annie.

Much.

"When we get to the Sugar Shack, somebody has to remind me to order fro-yo instead of ice cream," Lauren was saying. "I've been eating really healthily, and I don't want to blow it now!"

As the girls congratulated Lauren on sticking to her nutrition plan, Annie felt a rush of warmth. She knew how fortunate she was to have such a great, supportive group of friends.

Deep down, she knew one thing for certain: even if Sgt. Pepper might consider her a member of his Lonely Hearts Club, as long as she was a roller girl, she'd never, ever be truly lonely.

And *that* was the best Valentine's Day present she could ever ask for.

Chapter Nine

"Excuse me," said Dad, as Annie lugged yet another duffle bag down the front path, "but I was under the impression you were only going to be away for a few days."

"I am," said Annie, hoisting the heavy bag of skates and equipment into the trunk.

"Then why did you pack as if you'll be gone for a few *years*?"

"Dad, have you *seen* me after a skate practice?"

"Of course."

"Then you may have noticed that I tend to get a little sweaty."

Dad grinned. "True. It's actually pretty disgusting."

Annie didn't take offence. "And since I won't have time to do laundry at camp, I'm going to need fresh workout clothes for every day of the week." She scanned the three nylon duffle bags in the back of the truck. "I just hope I didn't forget anything."

"Did you remember your ankle brace?" asked Dad.

"Ankle brace, check," said Annie.

"Helmet?"

"Check."

"Mouthguard?"

"Check."

"Good, because you wouldn't want to borrow someone else's mouthguard."

"Gross."

"Very. Hmm, what else? Toothbrush, toothpaste, dental floss?"

"Check, check, check."

"Socks, pyjamas, and other unmentionable girly type undergarments?"

"Check, check, and awkward but yeah … check."

Dad laughed, climbing into the driver's seat. "Sounds like you've got everything," he said. "I think we're good to go."

"Wait!" cried Annie. "I did forget something." She turned and dashed back into the house, where she'd left a pile of CDs on her desk, and scooped up a handful.

"I thought we'd need tunes," she explained.

"Always thinking ahead, that's my Beanie!" Dad chuckled. "Do we need to pick Lexie up?"

"No," replied Annie. "She's meeting us at Rosie Lee's." The plan was to meet Lexie at the café and show her the ropes, so she could hold down the fort while Dad drove Annie to the university.

As Annie climbed into the passenger's seat, she was filled with a jumble of feelings. Mostly she was excited – pumped up about derby camp and ready to work as hard as she could. But she was also a little intimidated; she'd be skating with girls who were far more advanced than she was. She knew the whole point of camp was to improve, she just hoped she wouldn't make too poor a showing.

And there was something else, she realized, as she looked across the front garden at the colonial-style house that had once belonged to her grandparents. Annie was already feeling pangs of homesickness. It was silly, she knew, since she would only be gone for seven days. But she'd never been away from her father for that long before. For all his goofiness, he was truly the steadying force in Annie's world. She was going to miss him, even if it was only for a week. She knew Dad was feeling sad about it too, because he'd spent the whole morning being extra cheery to cover it up.

Annie would miss Lexie a lot as well. And as Holly was the only Belle who'd be attending camp with her, she'd also be missing her teammates.

And Jesse.

Just the thought of not being able to talk to him about, well, *anything*, really – from the artistic significance of the Ramones' *Road to Ruin* album to whether her skates would get better grip by switching her fifty-nine-millimetre wheels to sixty-two millimetres – actually sent a stab of panic to her heart.

That feeling took her by surprise. *Seriously?* she thought. *I don't like the Ramones* that *much*.

"All right, then," Dad said, slipping the key into the ignition. "Let's get this show on the road!"

"Let's do it!" chimed Annie.

Unfortunately, the truck had other plans.

Maybe it was due to the fact that she'd just that minute been thinking of him, or maybe it was because she knew he was a genius about anything with wheels.

Or perhaps it was simply that she wanted to say goodbye before she left town for a week. Whatever the reason, Annie's immediate thought was to call Jesse.

He was there in five minutes, surprising Annie by pulling up in his mother's car. She'd only seen him on his skateboard before.

"It sounded like an emergency," he said, by way of explanation. "I figured you wouldn't want to wait for me to roll here."

"Thanks for coming," said Annie. "I really appreciate it."

"No prob," said Jesse; then he got down to business, opening the bonnet and examining the truck's inner workings.

"So what do you think?" Dad asked.

"Definitely the fan belt," Jesse replied. "I think I could patch it up enough to get you started, but it would only be a temporary fix. I really wouldn't go much farther than the nearest service station with it."

Annie's heart sank. "How am I going to get to camp?"

"Maybe you can catch a ride with Holly's folks?"

Dad suggested.

But Annie shook her head, feeling the tears stinging behind her eyes. "They drove up yesterday to spend the night with family in the area." She frowned, thinking hard. "Could I take a taxi?"

"You could," said Dad. "Except the fare would cost more than I earn in a month at Rosie Lee's." He shrugged and shook his head, looking on the verge of tears himself. "I'm so sorry, Beanie."

"Um…" Jesse cleared his throat. "Maybe I can drive you."

Annie's eyes shot from Dad, to Jesse, then back to Dad. She felt a swell of hope. "Dad? Can he? Please?"

"Gosh, Annie, I don't know. It's a long way…"

"I'm actually a really cautious driver, sir," Jesse assured him. "I've only had my licence for six months, but I swear I'll be really careful."

Annie looked at her father with pleading eyes. *Say yes*, she implored. *Please, Dad. Say yes.*

Dad sighed, weighing up the options, but it was clear they had none. "OK," he said at last. "Jesse can drive you to camp."

"Oh!" Annie leaped into his arms and hugged him tight. "Thank you, Dad! Thankyouthankyouthankyouthankyou!"

It was a moment before Annie realized that although most of her joy stemmed from the fact that she wouldn't have to miss boot camp, she was also pretty pleased at the thought of spending the two-hour drive with Jesse. They'd have plenty of time to talk and catch up and just … well, hang out.

"Jesse," Dad was asking, "would you mind trying to do that

temporary fix you were talking about so I can get this old heap to a garage?"

"Sure thing, Mr Turner."

"Thanks. I'll go inside and call around to see where I might get the best deal on a fan belt."

"You should try Hank's Garage on West Avenue," Jesse suggested. "He's the only mechanic my mom trusts." He grinned. "Just tell him Jesse Mathieu sent you."

"Will do," said Dad, then turned to Annie. "You'll have to stop at Rosie Lee's on your way to let Lexie in and give her a quick tutorial on the opening routine. I'll be there later to teach her the rest of it."

When Dad disappeared into the house after giving Jesse some petrol money, Jesse walked around to the back of the pickup truck. He smiled when he saw the amount of luggage Annie was bringing.

"Guess you're not a fan of packing light," he joked.

Annie just smiled. She was not about to tell *him* she expected to spend the next seven days sweating like a pig!

He shifted her bags around, searching for something in the flat bed.

"What are you looking for?" she asked. "Tools? Owner's manual? Spare tire?"

"Why would I need the spare tire to fix a fan belt?"

Annie gave him an innocent look. "How should I know? That's why I called you."

"Actually, do you have an extra pair of tights in your suitcase?"

"You want a pair of my tights?" Annie echoed, confused.

"Not to wear," he said, smiling. "They're for the truck."

"Oh." Still confused, Annie dug into one of the duffles and pulled out her least favourite derby tights – a pair of black-and-red striped ones that had so many runs and tears in them they were practically fishnets. "Will these do?"

"Yep."

Ten minutes later, Jesse had fashioned a makeshift fan belt out of the tattered tights.

"Wow," said Annie, duly impressed. "You're amazing."

"Thanks."

"Who'd have ever thought my derby gear would also have automotive applications."

"Right?" Jesse laughed. "Just goes to show you how being a roller girl can serve you in all aspects of life."

Jesse transferred Annie's luggage into the Volvo's boot while she ran into the house to say goodbye to Dad, and then they were finally on their way.

As he guided the car cautiously towards Rosie Lee's, Annie couldn't help sneaking glances at him from her place in the passenger's seat.

He'd come to her rescue. Proud as she was to be a tough roller girl, she had to admit that getting in touch with her inner damsel was kind of fun. As she watched the muscles in Jesse's forearm flex when he shifted the gears, an interesting thought occurred to her.

Maybe a hero doesn't necessarily have to be a knight in shining armour riding a white stallion. Maybe sometimes, all you really need is a great guy in jeans and a Green Day T-shirt, driving his mother's Volvo.

Because Jesse had saved the day. He'd been there for her when she needed him. And Annie knew that even the most independent roller girl in the world couldn't argue with that.

Lexie looked confused when the blue estate car pulled up in front of Rosie Lee's with Jesse behind the wheel and Annie in the passenger's seat.

"Well, this is unexpected," she said, as they climbed out of the car.

"Look who's talking about unexpected," said Annie, taking in Lexie's attire.

Lexie did a little spin to show off her outfit. "You like?"

"I like!" said Annie, bobbing her head in approval.

True to form, Lexie had taken her temporary waitressing gig to the next level by going all out in the wardrobe department. She was wearing a snug-fitting, pink polyester dress, with an oversized collar and a scalloped white apron. There was even a little name tag pinned to the lapel that read "Dolores". She was also sporting a pair of cat's-eye glasses and a little paper crown on her head. She'd tucked a pencil behind her ear and had done her eyes up with old-school, powder-blue eyeshadow.

"I feel like we've just stepped back in time to 1957," laughed

Jesse. "Who's Dolores?"

"Dunno," said Lexie. "I guess she was the waitress who donated this vintage diner uniform to the thrift shop. Isn't it great?"

"It's brilliant!" said Annie. "My dad's gonna love it."

Lexie beamed. "Well, it was between this kitschy look, and a Victorian dress with a bustle, a pinafore, and a little lace mob cap. Technically, that would have been more in keeping with the whole British theme, but nowhere near as much fun."

"I think you made the right choice, Dolores," Annie giggled.

"Thanks, girlie," said Lexie, affecting a twang. Then she popped a piece of gum into her mouth and snapped it a few times. "So are yous two gonna show me around this dump, or what? I ain't got all day, and my feet are already killin' me. Jeesh, what's a gal gotta do to get a cuppa caw-fee in this joint, heh? And don't try to gimme any a' that new-fangled flavoured crap neither. A good old-fashioned cuppa joe, that's what I like."

Annie was cracking up as she unlocked the front door. She had a feeling that with a little help from "Dolores", Lexie would earn enough tip money to buy her new graphics tablet in no time!

Chapter Ten

After giving Lexie a crash course in opening Rosie Lee's and taking several scones and a handful of peanut butter cookies to eat along the way, Annie and Jesse were ready to get on the road.

"First things first," said Jesse, opening the console between the seats. He took out a homemade CD and popped it into the player. "Road rule number one: good tunes should always be a top priority."

As he pulled away from the curb, Annie tapped her foot to "Short Skirt/Long Jacket", one of her all-time favourite Cake tunes.

But her earlier excitement had given way to a mild case of anxiety. As comfortable as she and Jesse were with one another when they hung out at the rink, this was really the first time they'd ever been completely alone together. Ordinarily they just seemed to fall into witty banter, but all of a sudden, Annie found herself tongue-tied.

Maybe it was because there was no getting past the fact that sitting beside a boy in a car felt an awful lot like a date.

"This is kinda weird, huh?" said Jesse, reading her mind.

"A little," Annie admitted. "I guess."

"The only person I ever drive anywhere is my little sister, and she's too small for the front seat."

"Want me to hop in the back?" Annie asked without missing a beat. "Maybe change Cake for The Wiggles and I can start asking 'Are we there yet?' every five minutes."

Jesse laughed. And just like that, the anxiety was gone.

"You spend a lot of time with Katie, don't you?" asked Annie. She had met Jesse's little sister on Halloween night when he'd brought her trick or treating, and it was clear they had a great relationship.

"Yeah. I'm, like, a built-in babysitter, but I don't really mind. Katie's pretty cool for someone who still believes in the tooth fairy."

Now that Annie was able to relax she began to take in the scenery. Even though they'd been in Illinois for half a year, she'd seen very little of her new home state. She knew the charming streets and quaint neighbourhoods of Liberty Heights like the back of her hand. But that hadn't prepared her for what she was seeing now.

"It's beautiful! Practically all farmland," she observed, staring out of the window at the sprawling fields and wide-open land. In the middle of February, it wasn't exactly an inviting landscape, but the rolling meadows, sturdy barns, and old farmhouses that appeared every few miles had a kind of rugged beauty that Annie couldn't help but admire.

"I know this area pretty well," Jesse told her. "My grandparents live out this way and I used to spend my summers here when I was a little kid."

"That must have been amazing!"

"It was fun. One year there was this baby goat that followed me around constantly. Cute little guy, kind of clumsy and funny looking, but loaded with energy and very loveable." He shot Annie a sideways look. "I guess he figured we had a lot in common."

Annie laughed. "So when did you go from being a country boy to a skater boy?"

"I guess around the time my dad split." Jesse shrugged. "It was his parents who owned the farm, so naturally, things got a little weird for my mom after that."

"Sorry," Annie whispered. "I know how it feels."

"Yeah, I guess you do."

Annie realized this was the first time she and Jesse had ever talked about the subject of their parents' respective divorces. She was glad it had finally come up. It was comforting to discuss it with someone who understood first hand.

"Maybe I'll swing by and pay the g'rents a surprise visit on my way home," said Jesse.

"That would be nice. I'm sure they'd love to see you."

"Yeah. And I bet that goat has been wondering where the hell I've been, too!"

As they drove on, their conversation sailed smoothly from topic to topic, covering everything from embarrassing childhood anecdotes to current academic interests and favourite pizza toppings. The only thing Annie couldn't bring herself to ask Jesse was whether or not he had a girlfriend.

At one point, Annie's phone beeped. She checked the screen.

"Hope that's not Lexie, telling you she accidentally burned down Rosie Lee's."

"Nope. It's my mum."

Jesse smiled. "I like the way you say that – mum. What's she like?"

"Busy," said Annie, replying to Mum's "Have you arrived yet?" with an "Almost there!" and a smiley face. "She works constantly. Even when we lived in the same house, I barely saw her." Annie shifted in her seat and sighed. "And neither did Dad."

"I guess that would explain the split."

Annie nodded. "There was more to it, of course."

"My dad was pretty much the same way. Work came first. And not because he was concerned about supporting us. It was more about him feeling important and powerful. Once I asked him to come watch me at the skate park – I was just learning how to board slide, which is a pretty tricky thing to do, and I really wanted him to know I was getting good." Jesse gave a sad chuckle. "He spent the whole time checking stock reports on his phone. I could have fallen off the rail and busted my head wide open and he would've never even noticed."

"I'm glad you didn't," Annie said softly. "Bust your head open that is."

"Yeah." Jesse grinned. "Me too."

"Still, divorce sucks."

"No argument there." Jesse hit the indicator and veered off the highway onto a beautiful little country road. "You seem to be handling it pretty well, though."

"It's the new normal," said Annie. "What else can I do?"

Jesse hesitated before he answered. "You could go back to London."

Annie was so taken aback by his comment that she whirled to look at him with wide eyes. When he saw the hurt look on her face he quickly clarified, "Not for good. I was thinking more like a vacation. A visit."

"Oh."

"Did you really think I was suggesting you move back there? Like permanently?" He smiled and shook his head. "Because I'd hate that. I mean, I'd seriously hate that."

His tone was so sincere that Annie's heart actually fluttered. "You would?"

"Yeah. I would." He was blushing again.

Emboldened, Annie tilted her head and asked, "Why?"

"Well, for one thing, the Liberty Belles would be in big trouble without Anne R. Key in the line-up. And for another, you're the only girl I know who likes The Clash, the Sex Pistols, and Nirvana."

"That's true," said Annie. "So maybe if I do go back to London for a visit, you should come with me."

Jesse blinked. "Come to London with you?"

"Think about it! You could actually walk in the footsteps of David Bowie, Mick Jagger, and Ray Davies."

"That would be cool."

"And I'd take you on a guided tour of Camden Market! We could get matching T-shirts at Over the Top, and then we could stop by Cold Steel and get our eyebrows pierced."

"And *then*," said Jesse, laughing, "we could go straight to the US Embassy to see about revoking my citizenship, because if I *ever* pierced my eyebrow – or anything else for that matter – my mother would be waiting at the airport to *kill* me the minute I set foot on American soil."

"Fine." Annie rolled her eyes, pretending to be crushed. "No piercings."

"Glad to hear it."

"But what about everything else? You and me, rocking London town like it's never been rocked before?"

"Oh, I'm in," said Jesse, nodding emphatically. "I am *so* in."

It was all in fun, of course. A silly fantasy. They'd allowed themselves to get swept up in the make-believe. But what Annie realized, as she settled back in the passenger seat to watch the countryside slip by, was that she really could picture herself and Jesse together in London, having a blast.

Not only could she picture it, but somewhere deep down inside, she'd begun to wish for it, too.

* * *

They pulled into the quaint little college town an hour later and Annie was immediately charmed by the old brick buildings and tree-lined streets. College kids seemed to be everywhere, sipping tall coffees from cardboard cups, wrapped in Great Lakes University fleeces and hats.

"Nice place," said Jesse. "Looks like a page right out of the college brochure."

Annie looked at the campus map she'd downloaded from the internet. "Take a left at the traffic lights up there," she instructed, the excitement evident in her voice. Now that the proud domes and elegant spires of the university were visible, all traces of nervousness were gone. "I can't believe I'm about to enjoy a week of derby, all the time!"

"I knew you'd be a natural," said Jesse. "The first time I saw you bombing down Main Street on your inline skates. You almost took out poor little Sid Vicious."

"You said so," said Annie, remembering the moment Jesse's dog had caused her collision with Kelsey. "You said something like, 'Nice moves. You should be a roller girl.' I had no idea what you were even talking about."

"I think I actually said 'sweet' moves," Jesse said, grinning. "But I was right."

"Yes, you were," said Annie, her tone reverent. "And now I can't even imagine my life without derby. I can't explain how I feel when I'm on the track. It's as if I'm completely free.

Empowered."

"You don't have to explain it to me," said Jesse, a similar reverence in his voice. "It's the same for me with skateboarding. It's a chance to push yourself to your ultimate limit. To accomplish something that really matters to you."

Annie nodded, liking the fact that he understood. Then she pointed and said, "Veer right here, then turn into the second driveway on the left."

Jesse did as he was told. Unfortunately, instead of leading them to the student centre, where the camp-goers had been instructed to meet for registration, the second driveway brought them to the back of the science building.

"Oops," said Annie, as Jesse executed a perfect three-point turn. "I guess I misread the map. Try the third driveway."

But the third driveway took them to the outskirts of campus, to Fraternity Row – a street lined with stately old houses, each of which had large Greek letters attached to the front.

"I believe we've just found Party Central," said Jesse, eyeing a boy asleep on a decrepit sofa on the lawn outside one of the frat houses.

"Wow," said Annie. "Looks like someone had a rough night."

Annie consulted the map again, and was finally able to guide Jesse to the proper building. He pulled up to the curb and for a moment they both sat there, not sure what to do next.

"I don't want to make a bad first impression by being late to registration," said Annie, turning to face him. Her eyes met his and her next words came out in a whisper. "I guess I should go inside."

Jesse gave a little nod, but his intense blue eyes remained focused on hers. "Guess so."

In the close confines of the car Annie realized she could actually feel the warmth emanating from his skin; the light, clean scent of his shampoo filled the small space.

And his lips looked ridiculously soft.

She suddenly wanted to know *how* soft.

In the next heartbeat, she saw that he was leaning ever-so-slightly in her direction.

She was just about to mirror that action when a series of shrieks and giggles exploded just outside the car window. Annie jerked her head round to see a crowd of teenage girls running up the stairs to the student centre. They laughed and called out to another group of girls, who were hustling across the building's lawn to meet them.

Talk about mood-kill.

"The roller girls have arrived," Jesse observed with a chuckle.

Was it Annie's imagination or was there an undercurrent of disappointment in his laughter?

"Right. I should go in." She unbuckled her seat belt, still not ready to get out of the car.

But there was a steady stream of campers arriving now, so Annie forced herself to open the door. Jesse got out too and retrieved her three duffle bags from the boot.

"Have a great week," said Jesse. "Take no prisoners."

"I never do," Annie assured him. "Thanks for the ride.

Thanks for – " she smiled – "everything."

Feeling impulsive, she leaned over and gave him a hug.

"You're welcome," he said, close to her ear, sending a shiver up her spine.

Annie couldn't help but wonder what it would have been like if he had kissed her goodbye.

She sighed, deciding perhaps it was better that he hadn't. They were friends. A kiss would have just complicated things.

She waited on the pavement as he got back in the car, then watched as he drove away.

Annie felt desperately lonely for exactly one second.

Then she heard a familiar voice calling, "Yo, Anne R. Key!"

She turned to see Holly waving from the top of the student centre steps.

Boot camp was about to begin!

Chapter Eleven

An hour and a half later, after filling out forms and hearing some high-energy speeches from the Head Coach of the Illinoisies (who were sponsoring the camp) and a few of her team's veteran players, the thirty boot-campers were on their way to settle into a dorm.

The group was being guided by two young women who would be their counsellors and coaches for the next seven days. At registration, they'd been introduced to the campers by their roller derby names, Cherry Bomb and Mad Donna. They were both proud members of the local team, the Great Lakers, as well as the Illinoisies All-Star team. Cherry, who was fierce-looking, with purple hair and too many tattoos and piercings to count, looked to be in her early twenties. She was a graduate student right here at the university. Her counterpart, Mad Donna, was a bit older and worked as a librarian in one of the campus libraries. When the coaches had stood up to be introduced, Mad Donna had blushed and dipped her head demurely. Cherry, on the other hand, had flexed her inked biceps and let out a war whoop.

Annie laughed. To her, these coaches perfectly represented the opposite ends of the roller girl spectrum.

As they walked across the idyllic campus, Annie admired the manicured pathways and stately buildings.

Holly admired the boys. And, not surprisingly, the boys admired Annie's flame-haired friend right back.

They were walking with two girls Holly had befriended about three seconds after arriving at registration. Annie was glad she had Holly there – she wasn't sure if she'd have been bold enough to simply introduce herself to strangers as Holly had.

Their new friends were "Sue Nami" (real name Suzanne, she was originally from Alabama, but like Annie recently relocated to the Chicago area), and Luna Tortelli (a Jersey girl), whose derby name was "Luna Tick". They had met each other at a roller derby camp in Texas the summer before, and, like Annie and Holly, would be rooming together this week. Sue, with her long golden hair and porcelain skin, was exactly what Annie would have imagined a graceful Southern Belle to be. Luna was a dark-haired girl of Italian descent, who stood just shy of five feet and spoke with a thick Jersey accent.

"Hey, Legs," teased Luna, as a cute guy gave Annie the once-over in passing, "Joe College just checked you out big time."

Annie laughed. "How do you know he wasn't looking at one of you three?"

"Oh, he was definitely looking at you," Sue confirmed. "And Luna's right. He couldn't take his eyes off your legs."

Pint-sized Luna eyed Annie's long limbs, which were clad in a pair of skinny jeans. "I'd kill for stems like yours," she said. "How long are those babies, anyway?"

"Long enough to make her one of the best jammers here," said Holly.

The compliment took Annie by surprise. She smiled gratefully at her teammate.

"Well, Joe College was cute," Luna conceded, "but he's nothing compared to that boyfriend of yours."

For a moment, Annie was flummoxed.

Sue laughed at the expression on Annie's face. "She's talking about your ride," she explained. "The boy who dropped you off at orientation. We saw you in the car outside the student centre."

"Oh!" Annie giggled. "He's not my boyfriend."

Sue raised her eyebrows. "Why the hell not? He's ten different kinds of gorgeous."

"What would you know about that?" Luna said, laughing.

"I might be gay, but that doesn't mean I can't recognize a hot boy when I see one!" retorted Sue, punching her friend's shoulder affectionately.

"Oh," said Annie, blushing. "Jesse and I aren't dating. He's just a really good friend."

Both Sue and Luna turned doubtful looks to Holly, who just

shrugged and rolled her eyes.

By now, they'd arrived at their lodgings. The campers had been given the entire ground floor of a freshman dormitory. Great Lakes University held all kinds of programmes for high schooler pupils throughout the year – everything from Model UN conferences to chess competitions – so the housing department had a special floor devoted to hosting short-term visitors. Annie was glad she and the other girls would all be staying in close proximity to each other. It would make camp much more of a bonding experience. And not sharing a bathroom with college guys was a definite plus.

Cherry Bomb and Mad Donna read off the room assignments and distributed card keys. Annie was pleased to discover that the room she would be sharing with Holly was just across the hall from Sue and Luna.

"You will find a detailed camp schedule in your room," Mad Donna said in her sweet, efficient way. "Most of the clinics are mandatory, but there are also several skill-specific electives to choose from."

"We've provided campus maps as well," said Cherry Bomb. "Dinner will be in the south dining hall at six o'clock. That gives you plenty of time to unpack and get yourselves acclimated. A few late arrivals who missed registration will join us for dinner."

"Campers are also strongly advised to steer clear of the part of campus known as Fraternity Row," Mad Donna added in a serious tone. "It's populated primarily by upperclassmen, and since there's not a great deal of supervision there, we'd prefer you to avoid it."

To underscore her fellow coach's point, Cherry Bomb flexed her biceps again, as though to hint at the wrath that would be brought to bear upon any misguided camper who chose to break the rules.

Mad Donna gave the campers a serious look. "Boys will be boys, after all."

"And roller girls will be roller girls," Holly whispered with a grin.

Annie wasn't sure what Holly meant by that exactly, but decided not to press it. "Let's unpack," she said, tugging Holly towards their room. With any luck, Holly would forget about meeting college boys and Annie could focus on what she'd come here for.

Roller derby, roller derby, and more roller derby!

After making their beds, unpacking their clothes, and a quick stop at the campus bookstore (where Annie bought her dad a Great Lakes University T-shirt and treated herself to travel mug with the school logo) Holly and Annie arrived in the dining hall. The campers were assigned a handful of tables in a far corner, but there were plenty of university students there as well.

As Annie carried her tray she overheard two students having a lively discussion about Woody Allen's latest film. At another table she passed, a group of earnest-looking students were involved in a heated debate about third world debt. Annie found it thrilling and tried to imagine herself, four short years from now, living in a dorm and eating with friends in a college dining hall like this one. It seemed a completely different world to high school, where the main topic of conversation in the cafeteria was who was going out with whom.

"Eat up, campers," Cherry commanded. "We've got a big day planned for tomorrow."

Sue and Luna joined Annie and Holly at their table. Three other girls introduced themselves and sat down, too. They were Cheryl Madigan (Cher Madness), Carrie Ann Dempsey (Carrie A. Grudge) and Elle Sommers (Elle on Wheels).

The girls chatted pleasantly as they ate their dinner. When it was time to head back to the dorm, Annie picked up the remnants of her meal and followed the others to the tray-return.

As she made her way through the stream of college students, Annie was so entranced by the activity around her that she didn't notice the girl who had stopped short in front of her.

Annie's tray collided with the girl's back, and what was left of her cranberry juice spilled all over the back of the girl's shirt.

"Hey, what the—?" The girl spun to level a look at Annie.

They got the shock of their lives when each girl realized who the other one was.

"Figures it's *you*," snarled the girl who was dripping with cranberry juice. "The Duchess of Dork."

Annie scowled. "Dee Stroyer," she said dryly. "How lovely to see you."

Dee snorted, dropping her empty tray onto the conveyor belt and attempting to dry her shirt with a clump of napkins. "Shouldn't you be back in Liberty Heights baking cupcakes?"

"Actually, I thought my time might be better spent here," said Annie, breaking into a smile, "learning new and improved ways to kick your butt."

Holly, who was standing behind Annie, snickered.

Dee Stroyer glared, but for the first time seemed unable to come up with a snappy retort. With a glare, she turned on her heel and stomped out of the dining hall.

Luna gave Annie a pat on the back. "Way to spit game, Legs," she said, impressed. "Not bad, for a girl who ain't from Jersey."

"Let me guess," Sue giggled. "Friend of yours?"

"Hardly," sighed Annie. "More like my arch nemesis." The last thing she wanted was for her camp experience to be tainted by the presence of the mean-spirited Dee.

"Think of it this way," Luna advised as they exited the cafeteria. "Now you've got something to shoot for over the next week. Your goal is to make her life more miserable than she makes yours."

Annie gave her new friend a half-hearted smile. She knew Luna meant well, but to Annie's mind, derby wasn't about making someone else miserable. Competition was one thing – it made the game fun. But animosity was another thing all together.

As they headed back to the dorm in the chilly twilight, Annie looked around at the thirty or so other girls who were part of the boot camp. Maybe with so many roller girls around she'd be able to avoid Dee entirely.

She was certainly going to try! She only had one week here and she wasn't about to let anyone ruin it for her.

Annie had just pulled on the oversized Elvis Costello T-shirt she'd brought to wear as a nightshirt (having decided that her tattered Winnie the Pooh one was definitely not cool enough for derby camp) when there was a knock on the dorm room door.

She threw Holly, who was wearing checked fleece pyjamas, a curious look.

"Maybe it's those cute guys we talked to on the way back from dinner," Holly guessed, her eyes twinkling.

"God, I hope not," sighed Annie, opening the door a crack and peering out.

"Hi!" said Carrie Ann. "You guys up for some company?"

"Sure!" Annie swung open the door and beamed when she saw seven more girls in the corridor. "Come on in!"

She and Jesse had been so busy talking they hadn't touched the cookies and scones she'd brought for their drive, so she dug them out of her bag and set them on the desk. "Help yourself," she said, delighted that her and Holly's room had become the gathering spot.

In addition to Carrie Ann, their guest list included Sue, Luna, Elle, and Cheryl. Cheryl had brought along her room-mate, Eve, and the two girls from the room next to theirs, Ashley and Charlotte.

As the girls shared the baked goodies, they settled in around the room, flopping onto the beds, chairs, or the carpet. One of the first things Annie noticed was Charlotte's gorgeous, strawberry-blond curls. Charlotte had swept them up into a mass on top of her head. Long, red-gold tendrils bobbed around her face.

"I love your hair," said Annie. "It's such a pretty colour."

"Thanks," said Charlotte. "It's how I got my derby name … Ginger Snapped!"

This kicked off a discussion of how they chose their roller derby monikers. Annie was pleased when Ashley (who went by Ashes to Ashes on the track) guessed that the name Anne R. Key was a nod to the Sex Pistols song.

"Well, you're obviously from the UK," Ashley giggled. "It makes sense."

"Are you into punk?" Annie asked.

Ashley nodded. "My older brother doesn't listen to anything else," she explained, nibbling a scone. "I was singing along with the Dead Kennedys back in the fourth grade!"

"In Jersey, it's all about Springsteen and Bon Jovi," Luna said.

"Speaking of music…" Holly dug out her iPod and the girls started dancing around the room to Jay-Z's latest hit. Suddenly, there was a loud pounding on the door. The girls froze.

"Cherry Bomb?" Elle guessed in a whisper.

"We're dead," gulped Carrie Ann.

Holly turned off the music and opened the door.

But it wasn't an angry coach she found on the threshold.

It was worse. Much worse.

It was Dee Stroyer.

All ten girls gaped at her, as she stood there in her nightgown.

Annie felt a pang of pity for Dee, standing there alone – maybe she was homesick. Perhaps she'd knocked because she heard all the fun and wanted to be included. Annie was just about to open her mouth to invite her to join in, but Dee spoke first.

"Keep it down!" she barked. "Some of us are trying to rest up for tomorrow's workout."

"Sorry," Sue muttered.

"Don't be sorry," Dee spat. "Be *quiet*!" Then she left, slamming the door behind her.

Luna was shaking her head in disgust. "I think tomorrow I'm gonna have to open up a can of Jersey whoop-ass on that witch!"

"Good!" said Ashley. "She's got it coming. Can you believe she had the nerve to tell us off for having fun?"

Annie could definitely believe *that*. But what she *couldn't* believe – what had her in a complete and total state of shock – was what Dee Stroyer, the meanest girl Annie knew, had been wearing. The tough-talking roller girl slept in an old-fashioned pink satin nightgown with lace trim and ribbons!

"That was unexpected," Annie whispered to Holly.

"Yeah," Holly agreed. "I'd never have imagined Dee to be the frilly nightie sort."

Annie laughed, shaking the image of Dee's pink nightgown out of her head. Camp was turning out to be more of a learning experience than Annie had ever dreamed.

Chapter Twelve

The next morning, Annie awoke to the sound of her phone alarm. She was momentarily disoriented, unable to place the bare breeze block walls and institutional furniture.

Then it all came crashing back to her – where she was and why she was there – and she sat up in bed, grinning.

"Wake up!" she called out to Holly. "Camp starts in half an hour."

Holly groaned and rolled over, pulling the covers over her head.

It took some prodding, during which Holly begged for "five more minutes" of sleep, but finally Annie was able to rouse her room-mate.

She was glad to find Carrie Ann and the others waiting for

them in the corridor to go to breakfast.

Again, Annie got a huge thrill out of dining with the college crowd. She noticed that many of them looked exhausted and bleary-eyed.

"I guess they were all up late studying," Annie said.

"On a Saturday night?" Holly hooted with laughter. "I'm sure they were up late, but I doubt they were studying."

Annie noticed that the girls were getting several curious looks from the university students. Well, of course they were. They were all decked out in their derby gear – hot pants, colourful tights, and T-shirts with their derby names and numbers emblazoned on the back.

"Do you think they think we look silly?" Charlotte asked, her hand going self-consciously to her mass of strawberry curls.

"Who cares?" asked Holly.

"Good point," said Charlotte, laughing. She stared down a snooty-looking sorority girl and shook out her mane like an angry lion.

The girls had a quick breakfast, then hurried over to the gym, arriving right on time.

Annie scanned the group, and saw that, like herself and Holly, most of the girls had broken off into smaller groups.

All except for Dee. Dee stood alone.

For a moment, Annie almost felt sorry for her. But then Dee noticed her looking and shot her such a vicious look that Annie lost all sympathy. No wonder she was by herself. Frilly nightgown or no frilly nightgown, the girl was just too mean to make friends.

Cherry Bomb wasted no time getting things started. She assembled them all in the middle of the gym where there was a makeshift track marked out with electrician's tape. Then she held up a pack of playing cards.

"Ooh," joked Holly. "I love card tricks."

"Our first warm-up," said Cherry, smiling rather sinisterly, "is called Deck of Death. Each suit corresponds to a particular callisthenic. You'll each draw a card and whatever suit you get will determine which exercise you'll be expected to execute."

"Hearts are sit-ups," Mad Donna explained. "Diamonds are lunges, spades are jumping jacks, and clubs are squat thrusts."

This elicited a groan from the campers.

"Who wants to be the first victim?" asked Cherry.

Annie wasn't surprised to see Holly's hand shoot into the air. "I'm game," she said, stepping forward to join Cherry in the middle of the track.

Cherry spread the deck into a fan, and Holly plucked one from it.

"Ugh," she said, waving the seven of clubs for her camp-mates to see. "Seven squat thrusts."

"Let's go, ladies," barked Cherry, and Mad Donna gave a shrill blast of her whistle.

Obediently, the campers did the exercise – a deep knee bend to touch the floor, into a quick extension by kicking the legs back, then back to the squat position and exploding into an upward jump.

"That's one!" Mad Donna cried.

Again, the girls crouched, then planked, then propelled themselves upward.

"Two," Cherry counted off. "Five to go. Bend deep, jump high! Make it burn!"

"Oh, it burns all right," muttered Holly.

By the third squat thrust, Annie could feel her thighs sizzling. It was a good pain that signalled the strengthening of her muscles.

"Seven!" Mad Donna announced finally. A few of the girls crumpled dramatically to the floor, laughing. Others shook out their legs while breathing deeply.

Annie couldn't believe how strenuous the exercise was. *I thought I was in shape*, she marvelled silently. *This is harder than I thought.*

A girl from California went next and chose the three of diamonds. Three lunges. Nowhere near as challenging as the squat thrusts, but still tough.

Then Cherry pointed to Annie. "You're up, Anne R. Key."

Annie stepped forward and reached towards the deck. She drew, of all things, the Queen of Hearts, and immediately recalled the newspaper ad with the nasty message taped to her locker.

Apparently, she wasn't the only one who remembered.

"Way to go, Queen of Tarts," came a nasty voice from behind her.

Annie turned to see Dee smirking cruelly.

"Twelve sit-ups," Mad Donna commanded. "Everybody on the floor."

As the girls began counting out the dozen crunches, Annie pushed the memory of the newspaper prank out of her mind.

She had more important things to think about.

Like how to get through this crazy-difficult warm-up without collapsing!

Chapter Thirteen

At noon, Cherry blew her whistle and announced, "Lunch."

This was met with sighs of relief and more than a few shouts of sheer joy. The campers had been working steadily since their Deck of Death warm-up and everyone was exhausted.

Not to mention starving!

Mad Donna handing out the boxed lunches the dining hall had provided was one of the most welcome sights Annie had ever seen.

The girls took their little picnics and scattered themselves around the gym in small groups. Annie and Holly and the girls who'd hung out in their dorm the night before formed a cluster towards the top of the tiered benches.

Dee Stroyer sat with one other sullen-looking girl a few

benches down. They were close enough to Annie and her friends to include in conversation, but neither looked to be in the mood for friendly chit-chat. Dee and her reticent lunch partner made Annie feel glad that she and Holly had made so many new friends.

"Do they have roller derby in England?" Cheryl asked Annie.

"Yes," she answered. "But I'd honestly never heard of it until I moved here and my friend Lexie took me to see a bout."

"I remember going to see my first bout," said Luna with a nostalgic smile. "I was, like, six or seven, and my dad took me. My mom was always signing me up for things like dance and piano, but since I was about as musical as a rhinoceros, Pops thought maybe I should try something a little more athletic. We went to see the Jersey Jezebels play the Paramus Princesses and I was hooked after the first jam. Got my first pair of skates the next day."

"My older sister plays," Carrie Ann said, "so of course, I wanted to start as soon as I was old enough." She laughed. "Turns out I'm just as good as she is."

"Don't be so modest," said Cheryl. "You're not just as good as your sister, you're better than her and just about everyone in our league."

Carrie blushed. "Thanks, Cher."

Annie took an apple out of her cardboard lunch box and bit into it. "Are you guys teammates?" she asked.

Cheryl shook her head. "We play on rival teams, but we've gone to school together since first grade, so we've always been friends."

"When our teams skate against each other, we act like we're

117

mortal enemies," Carrie said, giggling.

Annie noticed that Sue had unzipped her hoodie and was sliding it off her shoulders. Annie was impressed with the vintage Metallica tank top underneath. But before Annie could comment on her new friend's taste in music, Holly gasped.

"Wow!" said Holly, her eyes going wide. "What happened there?"

Annie followed Holly's gaze to a huge splotch of purple on Sue's shoulder.

"It's a beauty, isn't it?" said Sue, beaming with pride. "I took a spill at practice two weeks ago. My coach thought I broke my collarbone, and my mother cried for days."

"She was probably afraid you did some real damage," said Elle, biting into her tuna sandwich.

"It wasn't that," said Sue. "She was worried the bruise wouldn't fade in time for me to rock the off-the-shoulder dress I'm supposed to wear to my cotillion next month."

"A roller girl debutante!" cried Annie. "That's brilliant."

The girls laughed, and Charlotte pulled down her stripey knee sock. "Check out this gash," she said, indicating a snake-like scar on her shin. "First bout of the season! Nine stitches."

For the next several minutes, it was all about scraped elbows, bruised ribs, and chipped teeth. And the best part was that each injury came with an exciting story.

When it was Annie's turn to show and tell, she didn't hold back at all. "I sprained my ankle right before Halloween," she said, rolling down her sock and showing her friends her ankle brace. "It swelled up like a pumpkin and I had to hobble around on crutches. I couldn't skate for two weeks!"

As she spoke, Annie shifted a purposeful glance at Dee, and was glad to see the bully flinch.

"Ouch," said Luna. "Crutches suck."

"How'd it happen?" asked Eve, popping a piece of a granola bar into her mouth.

"Well, let's just say it was a trick that didn't come with a treat," said Annie in a cool voice.

At that, Dee turned and scowled at her; Annie met her eyes without blinking.

"An opponent decided to play dirty," she went on. "I guess she thought she had no chance of out-skating me if she didn't take drastic measures."

"That's pathetic," said Carrie Ann. "I hate it when girls play dirty."

"Me too," said Sue. "I mean, sure … sometimes you have to get aggressive, but there's no excuse for poor sportsmanship."

"I couldn't agree with you more," said Annie, her eyes boring into Dee's.

Dee just sneered, not showing so much as a shadow of remorse.

Annie wasn't surprised. She'd expected that. Still, it felt good to be able to look Dee in the eye and tell her what she thought.

Maybe she was going to learn a lot more than just derby skills here at camp.

Maybe she was finally going to develop some real guts!

* * *

Annie was glad she'd eaten every last morsel of her boxed lunch, because the afternoon session required a lot of hard work and energy. It was all about agility and moves.

"Fancy footwork" was what Mad Donna called it.

She and Cherry Bomb set up an obstacle course and got the girls to run through as fast as they could … on their toe stops. This filled the gym with a thundering sound as the hard rubber stops stomped on the wooden floor.

"I know this camp is supposed to keep us on our toes," Annie giggled, "but this is ridiculous."

"We sound like a stampede of elephants," Charlotte remarked.

When they'd run the course six times, Cherry told them to relax. As the girls panted and wiped the sweat from their faces, Cherry explained the importance of "speed checks".

"This is so jammers don't crash into a slower-moving wall of blockers," she said. Then she went speeding around the track, her purple hair flying out from beneath her helmet.

"She's going to demonstrate a hockey stop," Mad Donna explained. "Watch carefully."

Cherry zoomed towards them, then twisted at the waist, swinging her knees and shins around while pushing her skate heels forward so that they were perpendicular to the direction she'd been heading. She stopped cold – arms out, knees bent. Annie imagined that if she'd been on an ice rink, her skate blades would have kicked up a shower of snow.

"Your turn, ladies!" said Mad Donna.

Cherry talked them through it. "Use your heels, and keep those knees soft. It's a smooth motion, not a jerk, but it's fast and hard. Concentrate on balance."

"Start skating," said Mad Donna. "When I blow the whistle, everyone try a hockey stop."

The girls set off around the track. When they'd built up sufficient speed, the coach let out a shrill blast.

Knees ... heels ... twist ... stop ... Annie let her waist swivel and her skates slam forward.

The next thing she knew she was flat on her back, dodging other first-time hockey stoppers, who were falling around her like snowflakes. At least a third of the campers hit the floor – some sprawled on their bellies, others landed backside first. A chorus of grunts and groans filled the gym.

Holly, of course, executed the stop flawlessly. Sue wobbled a bit, but managed to stay on her feet. Annie took some satisfaction in seeing Dee Stroyer go belly-up, but then felt angry with herself for being so spiteful. She hated that Dee brought out those feelings in her.

Sue glided over and offered Annie a hand.

"I think you're going to have bruise as bad as mine," said Sue, pulling Annie to her feet.

"I think you're right," said Annie, gingerly massaging her shoulder. "Lucky for me, I don't have any strapless dresses in my immediate future."

Mad Donna got them to try the hockey stop several more

times. Each time, there were less casualties littering the track, and by the fourth attempt, Annie had nailed it.

The next skill involved 180-degree turns. The coaches got the girls to sit in a semicircle and watch while they took turns demonstrating the many different ways of accomplishing an effective "about face". The turning options included hopping, dragging skates around, kicking up heels, and digging toe stops into the floor.

As the girls practised the various techniques, Annie focused on perfecting the sassy little hop turn. She repeated it again and again, making a complete 180 every time.

"That was awesome, Annie," Mad Donna called from across the gym. "You really nailed it."

Annie felt her cheeks flush with pride at the coach's praise.

Then Cherry blew her whistle to dismiss them for the day.

After a quick shower and a change of clothes, Annie gave Dad a quick call.

"Beanie!" Dad said when he picked up his phone. "How's my favourite roller girl in the world?"

"Boot camp is amazing!" Annie gushed. After filling Dad in on camp and her new friends, Annie noticed the time. "Dad, I've got to go – the dining room is closing soon and I don't want to miss dinner."

"Glad to hear you've got your priorities straight," Dad joked.

"I've got to run too; there are some gingerbread men in the oven who are in danger of being cremated."

After dinner, Annie and Holly met up with Cheryl, Eve, and Luna. Their other new friends had opted for an early night after the gruelling practice, but Annie was eager to get a better look at the campus and the surrounding area.

"Minus Fraternity Row," she reminded Holly pointedly.

Holly pouted but didn't argue.

They spent some time wandering around the quad, but as it was still snowy and cold, only a few students were out taking advantage of the broad stretch of lawn centred in the middle of classroom buildings and dormitories. Annie loved the gorgeous old buildings, and even suggested a quick tour of the enormous library, but Luna just laughed.

"I see enough books during school. This is vacation."

Annie decided she couldn't argue with that, and after a brief visit to the vast arts centre, where they watched a bit of a choral group's rehearsal and admired some of the student artwork displayed in the gallery, the girls headed off campus to see what the Main Street had to offer.

In a word: everything!

There were second-hand bookshops, clothing boutiques, cool restaurants, even an art-house movie theatre. Eve wanted to stop in the yogurt shop for a smoothie, but Holly had a better idea.

"Check it out," she said, pointing across the street to a place called Ziggy's. "That place looks like fun."

Every time the door opened for someone to enter or exit,

the girls could hear the sound of cheers and loud music coming from within.

"Perfect!" said Luna. "The sign says 'Battle of the Bands'."

They all hurried across the street and stepped inside, where there were candlelit tables and the smell of strong coffee.

"A coffee shop with live music," said Cheryl. "This is *so* cool."

"Right?" said Holly, guiding them towards an empty table, close to the small, raised platform that served as a stage. Five girls in matching gold lamé miniskirts and high heels were clamouring off the stage after their performance.

A guy in a Great Lakes University T-shirt bounded onto the platform. "Give it up for The Stilettos!" he cried, his voice booming through the microphone.

The room rippled with half-hearted applause.

"Looks like they aren't going to win this battle," Holly observed. "But I give them major props for gold lamé. Maybe when they realize they have no future in music, they can try roller derby."

"Five espressos," Luna told the waitress, who appeared the minute they were seated. "With a lemon twist."

When Annie eyed her curiously, Luna shrugged and giggled. "That's how my grandfather takes his espresso," she confessed. "I have no idea if it tastes good or not."

It didn't, Annie concluded, the moment the steaming black liquid touched her lips. It was strong and bitter and the lemon rind straddling the rim of the tiny cup did nothing to improve the flavour of the beverage. At Rosie Lee's they served plenty of coffee – but never with lemon! She noticed the other girls wincing as they tasted theirs as well, but no one wanted to seem immature by admitting they didn't like it.

Annie looked around. The place was crowded for a Sunday evening, and the rest of the clientele was made up of college students. She guessed they had come here to support their friends, battling for the title of Coolest College Band.

The next contestants were four extremely hot guys, who called themselves Dirt.

"This is so cool!" Annie breathed.

"Yeah," Holly agreed, as Dirt launched into a funky fusion of jazz and rock. "Don't see much of this back in Liberty Heights."

That was the truth. Annie began taking mental notes, determined to get the details exactly right when she told Jesse about it at home next week.

Jesse. The thought of him sent a pleasant shudder up her spine. How amazing would it be to be sitting here sipping coffee with him, listening to the music and…

"Hi."

Annie was jarred out of her daydream by a deep voice over her shoulder. She turned to see four cute college boys seating themselves at the table behind theirs.

"Oh," said Annie. "Hi."

The boy who had spoken to her was tall, with wavy blond hair and clear blue eyes. He had broad shoulders beneath a navy blue crew neck sweater.

"Have you heard these guys?" he asked, motioning to the

quartet. "They're incredible. They've got a really unique sound."

"I'll have to take your word for it," said Annie, smiling. "I don't really know much about jazz."

"Well, you've come to the right place if you want to learn." The boy smiled warmly. *Very* warmly. "I'm Todd, and I'll be happy to answer any musical questions you may have. That is, if you answer a question of mine first."

Annie gulped. Was this college boy flirting with her? "OK," she squeaked.

"Aren't you in my World History seminar?"

"Um…" Annie shook her head. "No. I'm definitely not."

"Too bad." He smiled. "Are you a sophomore?"

"That's two questions," said Annie, smiling back. "But no, I'm just a freshman." She was about to add *in high school*, when Holly piped up.

"She doesn't take World History," said Holly. "She's an Econ major. And so am I."

Annie whirled to stare at Holly with wide eyes. *Since when?* she wanted to ask.

But Cheryl, Eve, and Luna seemed more than willing to go along with Holly's charade. As Annie listened in shock, Cheryl informed the boy that she was pre-med. Eve claimed to be a double major in Spanish and Psychology, and Luna, it turned out, was still undeclared.

Whatever that meant.

"I'm pre-law," said the boy next to Todd, whose soccer jacket had the name "CHAD" embroidered on it. He was a little stockier than Todd. "But I switched majors three times." He couldn't seem to take his deep, dark eyes off Holly. "I guess I just couldn't make up my mind, so I tried a little of everything."

"Well, they say variety is the spice of life," Holly purred, with a flutter of her eyelashes.

One of the other boys chuckled and said something to Eve in flawless Spanish. Eve didn't appear to have any idea what he'd said, but she smiled so sweetly the boy didn't seem to notice his comment had been lost in translation.

Luna laughed and ordered another round of coffees – lattes this time, thankfully.

Annie was beginning to feel a nervous knot forming in her gut. Lying about their age to college boys seemed like a really bad idea.

But then the music started up again, and the café was filled with the rhythmic thump of a bass and the rasp of a snare drum, and she decided not to worry. It was just a harmless flirtation.

Seriously … what harm could come from that?

Chapter Fourteen

The next morning, when Annie's phone alarm pierced the silence of the dorm room, the last thing she wanted to do was get out of bed.

"Five more minutes," she groaned to Holly.

"Five?" Holly echoed. "I was gonna ask for fifteen."

They settled on ten, which became twenty, and when they finally rolled out from under the covers (no easy feat, considering every muscle in Annie's body was stiff and sore from yesterday's workout) they found themselves in a major rush.

Annie grabbed her shower kit, then made her way painfully to the shared bathroom to brush her teeth and splash water on her face. As she bent over the sink, she cringed at the dull ache in her quadriceps and calves. Her shoulder was tender where she'd landed on it yesterday and her abdominal muscles throbbed. But she wasn't going to complain; she knew that pain in the present would result in strength in the future. This was exactly what she'd come here for.

When she got back to her room, she found Holly – wide awake now – tearing the place apart. Annie gaped at her room-mate, who was digging through drawers and duffle bags, manically flinging clothing around the room.

"What are you doing?" Annie asked, dropping her toothbrush on the bed and ducking a trainer that came flying across the room.

"Looking for my pads," said Holly. "They're gone."

"How can they be gone?"

Holly dropped to her knees to search under one of the beds. "That's a good question! I put them in my gym bag after practice, and haven't touched them since. But somehow they've vanished."

Annie frowned, then crossed the small room to unzip her own gym bag. Her skates and helmet were right there where she'd left them, but her elbow and knee pads where nowhere to be seen.

"What the—?"

"Yours too?"

Annie nodded. Then she opened the two drawers she'd claimed for her own and rifled through them, tossing shirts, shorts, and socks around the room like confetti. When the pads didn't turn up, she pulled the sheets and blankets off her bed, on the off chance that they had somehow got tangled up in the bedding.

No luck.

Holly bounded to her feet and yanked open the wardrobe. But as it was basically empty except for the few non-workout outfits the girls had hung inside, it was immediately apparent that their pads were not there either.

"Maybe we just forgot them at practice," Annie suggested. "Maybe we left them behind in the locker room by mistake."

Having no other choice, the girls gave up the search and rushed to get dressed. They missed breakfast entirely and headed straight to the gym ... late and padless.

Cherry eyed them as they joined the group, clicking her tongue in disgust.

"Do you girls show up late for bouts at home?" she chastised. "Not a very admirable quality in a roller girl."

"We're sorry," said Annie. "We would have been on time except..." She looked down at her skates, mustering up her courage. "We couldn't find our pads. We both thought they were in our derby bags, but when we went to find them they were gone. I guess we both misplaced them."

Out of the corner of her eye, Annie noticed Sue and Luna exchanging glances. Carrie Ann was shaking her head and Eve was frowning. Annie suddenly realized what they were thinking – now that she'd heard herself say it out loud, she realized what an unlikely coincidence that was. She was always very careful with her equipment, and she knew Holly was practically obsessive about hers. Neither of them would simply misplace something as important as their pads. What were the chances of both of them leaving their stuff behind?

Pretty slim, she decided.

She was about to suggest to the coaches that perhaps someone had stolen them when Mad Donna pointed to a small pile of pads.

"Someone turned those in this morning."

"Those are ours," said Annie sheepishly, recognizing her protective gear.

"Well, then," said Mad Donna. "You should be very grateful that someone was kind enough to hand them in."

Holly glared at Dee. "I think the bigger issue is how they went missing in the first place."

"I agree," snapped Cherry Bomb, missing Holly's inference entirely. "Roller girls should be organized and responsible. Which means looking after their equipment and arriving at practice on time."

As Annie and Holly collected their pads, Annie felt a slow burn beginning in her belly. She knew, as did Holly, that Dee Stroyer had to be the one who'd sneaked into their room and stolen their pads – and then turned them in like a Good Samaritan, just to score points with the coaches. Clearly, she'd graduated from taking cheap shots on the track to playing dirty off of it. Annie realized that she and Holly were going to have to watch their backs.

Once they were all suited up, they joined the rest of the campers for the morning's first drill.

"Black Widow," Cherry Bomb announced. Then she

proceeded to describe the exercise, which involved one full minute of skating, while executing a single skill, such as skating backward, or weaving, or doing figure of eights.

"How bad can that be?" Annie asked naively. "It's only one minute."

Luna Tick laughed. "A minute is a lot longer than you think, Legs."

When the whistle blew, Annie took off with the pack, choosing weaving as her Black Widow skill. Cherry Bomb shouted out pointers while Mad Donna watched the clock.

At the end of the sixty seconds, Annie was absolutely exhausted!

Cherry led them in a few more drills including one of Annie's favourites, the Bus Driver. Then they broke the group up into teams and had a scrimmage.

As one of the youngest players, Annie was on the bench for the first two jams, but she was a blocker in the third jam. Finally, in the fifth jam, she was jammer and scored five points. Holly made an impressive showing as well, and Sue Nami proved herself to be an amazing blocker. It was exhilarating and inspiring to play with such talented girls.

At noon, the girls were sent to the dining hall for lunch.

As they made their way along the path through the chilly air, Annie noticed that Holly had a very determined look on her face.

"What are you thinking?" she asked.

"I'm thinking that nobody makes a fool out of me and gets away with it," she hissed, her eyes searching out Dee, who was walking alone further ahead on the path. "And I'm thinking I need to point that out to that witch … right now."

"Holly…" Annie began in a warning voice.

"Don't do anything you'll regret," Cheryl cautioned.

"I don't think Holly Terror knows the meaning of 'regret'," Sue giggled.

Annie was afraid there was more truth to that joke than Sue realized.

Holly took a deep breath and marched ahead of the group. She came around in front of Dee, stopping the bully dead in her tracks.

"Hey!" Holly barked.

Dee looked down her nose. "Get out of my way, midget."

Holly ignored the order. Annie and the others had caught up to them now, and Annie was close enough to see that the look Holly gave Dee was one of pure fury.

"I'm only going to say this once, Dee. If you ever mess with my or Annie's stuff again, you're gonna be very sorry."

"Really?' Dee snorted. "Is this a threat?"

"Hell yeah," Holly growled, stepping closer. "A threat, and a promise."

Annie saw a flicker of concern pass over Dee's face, but she shook it off quickly. "Who says I took your stupid pads?" she huffed. "It's not my fault you Liberty Belles are too busy having fun to keep track of your equipment."

"Well, then it won't be my fault if my right fist just happens to connect with your face."

Then Charlotte was frantically clearing her throat and Annie turned to see the two coaches heading towards them on the path.

"Holly," Annie whispered, "we're already on the you-know-what list for being late. Please don't make things worse by getting in a fight!"

Holly gritted her teeth, but stepped away. Without another word, Dee stomped towards the dining hall.

Luna draped an arm over Holly's shoulder. "Excellent use of self-control there, girlfriend," she said. "I woulda belted that bi-atch right in her big mouth."

"Violence is never the answer," said Sue, batting her lashes as her voice dripped with a sweet Southern twang.

"Then what is?" Holly grumbled.

Sue smiled. "Revenge."

Annie laughed along with the rest of the group, but deep down she was beginning to get worried. This rivalry with Dee was getting out of hand and she didn't want things to go any further than they already had.

"Now that we've avoided a major throw-down right here on the quad," said Eve, "can we please grab lunch? I'm starving."

"Yes," said Annie. "Let's." *As long as we sit as far away from Dee Stroyer as possible*, she added silently.

The afternoon session was all about "juking", which Annie learned was the derby word for "faking". When done well, juking was a skill a roller girl could use to get past a particularly tough blocker.

The coaches asked for volunteers and assisted in demonstrating the many techniques associated with juking. This consisted of a combination of moves – bobbing up and down, side to side, and forward and back – performed in an effort to mislead the opponent into expecting one action when really, the plan was to do the exact opposite.

Annie was thrilled. She had been in countless situations in which she'd been stuck behind a blocker. If she could nail this juking business, she'd never have to worry about that problem again.

The volunteers struggled the first few times, but Cherry and Mad Donna patiently guided them through the technique. When the demonstration was over, the coaches paired the campers off to work on the skill.

Annie's heart sank when she found herself teamed up with her arch nemesis. Dee would be the blocker and Annie would have to use the faking methods to get past her.

As they sped around the track, Annie tried everything she'd seen the coaches and the volunteers do. She bent up and down and hopped from side to side, determined to better her rival. But Dee was just as keen not to let Annie get past.

Finally, Annie flung her hand out to the right side of Dee's head.

Dee immediately veered right, assuming Annie was heading in that direction, and Annie deftly swung out to the left of Dee, zooming past her effortlessly.

"Excellent hand fake, Anne R. Key!" Cherry Bomb called across the track. "Quick thinking, good skating. Nice work!"

Annie was delighted. She'd successfully faked out Dee, proving that when it came to being sneaky, she could be just as clever as her nemesis. But in Annie's case, she did it while playing by the rules.

Maybe from now on Dee would think twice about messing with the Liberty Belles!

When the session was over, the girls headed back to the dorm across the snowy campus. As they passed an old stone chapel, they noticed a group of boys wearing matching blue blazers assembling under one of the covered arches.

"What do you think that's all about?" Charlotte wondered. "Political protest?" Sue giggled. "Activists rarely wear matching coats."

Seconds later, they had their answer. The handsome group had arranged itself into a semicircle. One of the boys stepped forward and blew into a pitch pipe.

Suddenly, the most beautiful voices Annie had ever heard were ringing in perfect harmony through the dusky air.

"It's an *a cappella* group!" cried Eve. "They're incredible."

The girls listened to the impromptu concert in awe. To Annie's delight, the group was singing a fabulous version of

Talking Heads' "Road to Nowhere". The upbeat tune lent itself perfectly to the boys' vocal talents.

Instinctively, she pulled out her phone and filmed the performance. Then she sent the video to Jesse, with a text message that read: "Talking Heads go to college! Boot camp is wicked!"

Her fingers hesitated over the keys as she briefly debated whether to add "miss you". Then the song ended and the spectators burst into hearty applause. Annie quickly hit send so she could clap along with the crowd. But as the girls reluctantly pulled themselves away from the concert, Annie had a warm feeling knowing that Jesse would get to enjoy the musical treat too.

It was almost as good as if he'd been there to hear it with her. Almost.

Chapter Fifteen

It was unbelievable to Annie how fast the week went by.

The days were long and gruelling and wonderful. She could feel herself improving, with positive changes to her skating, strategizing, and technique. Every day she felt closer to the new friends she'd made and this only confirmed for her what she already knew: getting involved in roller derby was one of the best choices she'd ever made.

Finally, Friday dawned – the last full day of camp. On Saturday morning, the girls would be packing up and heading home.

The mood in the gym was bittersweet, as everyone was both looking forward to seeing their families, but dreading saying goodbye to their new coaches and friends.

They scrimmaged, pulling out all the stops to show off the skills they'd perfected over the last six days. Annie and Holly were on the same team, and they quickly found their rhythm, working together towards the singular goal of keeping Dee's team from winning. Deep down, Annie knew her desire to beat Dee was a bit petty – it should have been more about the team and the bout itself than a personal grudge match – but it still felt good to use her new juking skills to break through the pack again and again.

It was a resounding victory for Annie's team. She and Holly high-fived themselves silly while Dee skated off to a corner and fumed.

Lunch was boxed sandwiches in the gym again, and this was followed by watching a video of the scrimmage they'd just played.

Cherry and Mad Donna hit pause every three seconds it seemed to point out a specific move or skill. Annie realized soon enough that in the warm-hearted spirit of the final day, the coaches avoided highlighting mistakes and were mostly pointing out positive things, halting the film to give credit for a great block or some skilful skating move. Annie found this touching, especially as many of their compliments were for her exceptional juking. Mad Donna had only one constructive criticism for her, reminding her that the 180-degree turn they'd worked on a few days earlier would have come in handy after one particular block. Annie wasn't hurt or offended; in fact, she welcomed the instruction and made a mental note of it, knowing she'd remember it when the Liberty Belles' season resumed in the autumn. Or, with any luck, even sooner if she was lucky enough to get chosen for Coach Ritter's All-Star team.

Cherry pointed out a few of Holly's exceptional jams, and also Sue Nami's "greatest hits", before turning off the film.

And then, it was over. Except for that night's farewell party, camp was officially over.

Annie was surprised to feel tears spring to her eyes when Mad Donna announced, "That's all, ladies. You've all done a great job this week. Thanks for coming."

Even more surprising was the fact that the rough-and-tumble Cherry Bomb actually choked up when she said, "It's been a pleasure and a privilege, girls. I'm proud to know you all. If this is the future of roller derby, then the future looks pretty bright to me!"

When Annie glanced over and saw Holly brushing a tear from her cheek, she had to smile. That was the best thing about being a roller girl, she realized. You needed to have strong muscles and a tough attitude, but that didn't mean you couldn't have a soft heart, too.

That night, the girls sported their best non-workout clothes to attend their farewell dinner. It was being held in a snack bar that took up the entire basement of the library. Annie loved the name of it: Snacks In The Stacks. The menu consisted of piping hot pepperoni pizza, foot-long subs and cheeseburger sliders.

"It's a carb fest," Annie remarked, giggling. "But considering we worked off, like, eighty zillion calories this week, I'm not too worried about it."

Holly demonstrated her agreement by chomping into a roast-beef sub, chased down with a handful of nachos.

Phones were buzzing around the room like mosquitoes as girls weepily exchanged contact information. Promises to keep in touch took on the feeling of solemn oaths, and Annie was sure that they would be honoured. She herself had every intention of staying in close contact with Charlotte, Eve, Cheryl, Luna, and Sue.

Especially Sue...

As she watched her new friend help herself to a soda, an idea struck her. "Are you by any chance seeing anyone at the moment?" Annie broached.

Sue sipped her drink and gave Annie a curious look. "No. Why?"

"Well, I've got this friend, Lauren. She's great." Annie punched the screen of her phone until a photo of herself and Lauren popped up.

Sue smiled. "Cute."

"Right?" Annie felt a rush of excitement at the thought of introducing two people she liked and admired. "She's only just come out – in fact, she's not here because she was planning to tell her parents this week."

Sue winced. "I remember that experience. It was complicated to say the least."

"I was thinking maybe I could put you two in touch and she could talk to you about it," said Annie. "And then, ya know ... maybe..."

"Maybe we'll hit it off?" Sue finished, giggling.

"Yes!"

"Sounds good to me," said Sue, lifting her drink can to click Annie's cup of lemonade in a toast. "If she's a friend of yours, I like her already."

"Look at you playing matchmaker," teased Holly, sidling up with a slice of pizza.

Annie's heart flipped. She hadn't known Holly was in earshot, and now she felt terrible. Telling Sue, who was from out of town, was one thing, but maybe Lauren wasn't ready to share this information with the rest of her teammates yet.

Her panic must have been evident, because Holly gave her an understanding look.

"Don't worry, I already knew. Lauren told me last week. In fact, she's telling everybody on the team, one at a time. So it's OK. You didn't accidentally out her."

Annie breathed deeply, feeling relieved, but she made a mental note to be more careful when it came to discussing personal topics – especially when they concerned another person. Then she smiled at Holly. "Don't you think Sue and Lauren would get along brilliantly?" she asked.

"I do," said Holly. "They'd be a great couple." She bit into her pizza and grinned. "Kinda like you and Jesse."

Annie rolled her eyes. "This again? I told you—"

"Oh, I know what you told us," said Holly. "But I also know what I can see with my own eyes. And I think you two would be great together. Hell, you already *are* great together. You just don't know it yet."

Annie was spared further commentary on the topic by the arrival of two familiar faces. Todd and Chad, the boys from the jazz café, were entering the snack bar.

Eve was at Annie's elbow in a second flat, looking excited and panicked. "It's the boys from Ziggy's!" she whispered. "If they see us with the other campers, they'll know we lied about being students here."

"Maybe they won't notice us," said Annie.

"Too late," said Sue, motioning with her drink can. "They already have. And they're coming this way."

Holly gulped down the mouthful of pizza she'd just taken and turned a glowing smile at the boys.

"Hey," said Chad, his dark eyes sliding over Holly appreciatively. "It's the music fans."

"We just came down for a slice of pepperoni," said Todd, glancing around the room. "But what's with all the high school girls? Are we under attack?"

He had directed his question to Annie. She was going to have to think fast.

"Um … yeah," she stammered. "I think they're here for some kind of sports camp."

Chad surveyed the room. "Cheerleading maybe?"

"No!" snapped Annie. "Definitely *not* cheerleading."

"Roller derby," said Holly. "I, uh, I was talking to one of them when I was in line for pizza."

Annie braced herself, waiting for the boys to make some negative remark about roller derby, but no such comment was made.

"We were just studying upstairs and came down for a bite," Eve fibbed. "We were as shocked as you were when we found the whole place crawling with *youngsters.*"

Annie shot her a look. *Youngsters? Really?*

But Todd and Chad clearly thought she was making a joke and laughed.

"Well, I'm getting out of here," said Todd. "High school girls are jail bait."

Annie had no idea what that meant, but since Chad laughed, she laughed too. So did Holly and the others.

"Hey," said Chad, moving closer to Holly. "Our frat house is throwing a rager later on tonight."

Another term with which Annie was unfamiliar. "Rager?" she echoed.

"Yeah, it's gonna be huge," Todd informed her. "Live band, big dance floor, twenty kegs, and all the jello shots you can handle."

"Oh." Annie stiffened. She did not like the definition of "rager" at all.

"So…" Chad gave Holly a seductive look, then nodded towards Annie. "How about when you and your leggy friend here are finished chaperoning this Brownie meeting, you come

144

on over to Fraternity Row and join us?"

There was something about his voice that made Annie very nervous. She opened her mouth to decline on behalf of the group, but Holly was quicker off the block.

"That sounds awesome!"

"Great," said Todd, then leaned down to whisper in Annie's ear. "I've never hooked up with an Econ major before. Maybe you and I can fix that tonight."

Annie couldn't think of anything she'd rather do *less*.

But Holly clearly felt differently. "Just let us know what time," she said as smoothly as if she made plans to party with college guys every day. "We'll meet you there."

"Perfect." Chad told her the name of his fraternity and that she should show up around eleven.

Todd actually winked at Annie before he turned to leave. Wow. This guy could give Tyler lessons in cockiness! She had thought Todd was cute when she met him in the café, but now she realized he was just an older, more arrogant version of the boy she'd recently split up with. She wouldn't dance with him if he were the last World History major on earth!

"He seems to have a thing for you, Legs," Luna observed.

"Not interested," said Annie, then turned to give Holly a hard look. "You're not serious about attending this frat party, are you?"

"Why not?"

"Well, first of all, the coaches forbade us from even setting foot on Fraternity Row. They said it was dangerous. And second of all, did you hear the party menu? Booze, booze, and more booze."

"We don't have to actually drink any of it," said Holly. "We can just dance and have fun." She glanced around the group with a hopeful expression. "You guys in?"

There was an awkward silence.

"Technically," said Sue, "only you and Annie were invited."

"It's a frat party, not a cotillion," Holly laughed. "I don't think you need a formal invitation."

Sue shrugged. "It really doesn't sound like my thing."

"It totally sounds like my thing," said Luna, "but I spent half of last semester grounded for sneaking in after midnight. The last thing I need is to get caught at a frat party. My folks'll hold me prisoner in my room until graduation."

The others made similar excuses, citing sore muscles, unpacked suitcases and long journeys home in the morning. But Annie saw right through these alibis. They all knew the frat party was a bad idea and they didn't want any part of it. They were just as scared as she was.

"Well, we've got until eleven o'clock to decide," said Holly breezily, munching her pizza crust. "Let's make a decision then."

With that, the girls returned to the business of gathering phone numbers, email addresses, and Twitter names. But Annie was uneasy. She hoped by the time the farewell party was over and eleven o'clock rolled around, Holly would come to her senses and decide to blow off the frat party.

She managed to choke down a couple of sliders and half a piece of veggie pizza, but even the good food didn't make her feel better.

If Holly was determined to attend that party Annie knew there was no way she was going to stop her.

And that didn't seem like a good idea at all.

At ten thirty, the farewell dinner ended and the campers headed back to their dorm. The others went inside, but Holly kept walking in the direction of the frat houses. She paused when she realized Annie was no longer beside her.

Holly turned to eye Annie, who was standing fretfully on the path.

"You're coming with me to the party, aren't you?" asked Holly.

Annie glanced back towards the dormitory. "To be honest, I don't really want to. I think it's risky. Those boys are strangers. And they don't know we're – ..." she bit her lip, trying to remember Todd's phrase – "jail bait."

Holly rolled her eyes. "We'll be fine," she assured Annie.

"What if we get caught?"

"So what?" said Holly with a shrug. "What are they gonna do? Send us home? Camp's over. We're leaving tomorrow anyway." She backtracked along the path, and took Annie's hand. "Please, Annie. I really like Chad. I'm never going to meet a boy that cool in Liberty Heights. After all the hard work this week, we deserve to have some fun. I'll just dance and flirt a little."

Annie sighed. Holly was making it sound harmless.

And didn't Annie owe it to her to go along? After all, Holly had stood up to Dee on Annie's behalf. They were teammates, and teammates stuck together, no matter what. Coach Ritter's words echoed in her head: "*If you let your teammate down, you let yourself down.*"

"Think of how impressed Lauren and Liz and Sharmila will be when we tell them we actually went to a frat party!" Holly coaxed. "And I'm sure Jesse will think it's the coolest thing ever."

Annie did like the idea of Jesse knowing she'd done something slightly wild. After all, what good was listening to all those punk rock anthems she loved so much, if she wasn't going to go a little crazy when she got the chance?

"One hour," Annie said at last. "We leave at midnight on the dot."

"Just like Cinderella," Holly laughed.

"Right," grumbled Annie, following along as Holly tugged her down the path towards Fraternity Row. Secretly, though, she had the feeling that if Cinderella had been invited to the ball by a frat boy instead of a charming prince, she would have kicked off her glass slippers and stayed at home!

Chapter Sixteen

Omega Alpha house was easy to find. Every light in the place was on and music blared from the open doors and windows.

Holly quickened her step when she saw it, but Annie wanted to turn and bolt.

"One hour," Holly reassured her, dragging her onward.

College kids streamed in and out of the enormous Victorian house. Boys and girls clung to each other, kissing on the front porch or pressed up against tree trunks. Annie could actually smell the beer from the pavement!

What had she got herself into?

Holly seemed to have no such worries. She pulled Annie up the front steps, skipping over a guy who was passed out cold, and into the crowded house.

"Isn't this amazing?" Holly shouted over the din.

Annie had to admit, the energy was infectious. The band was rocking hard and beautiful people were dancing together under a strobe light. Everyone looked happy and carefree. Maybe if she relaxed a little, she'd actually have fun.

"Let's find the keg," Holly suggested. "That's probably where Chad is."

Well, that certainly seemed like sound reasoning to Annie. She pushed her way through the crowd behind Holly, tightly grasping her friend's sleeve. They found the keg in what must have been the dining room of the old house. A girl was doing a handstand on it and her friends were cheering her on.

One of those friends was Chad.

"You made it!" he cried when he spotted them. Annie took some comfort in the fact that he seemed genuinely glad to see them.

"Wouldn't miss it," Holly replied.

"Need a drink?"

Annie shook her head. She knew the legal drinking age was twenty-one in the US. She'd broken camp rules by coming to the party on Fraternity Row; she didn't want to tempt fate by breaking the law as well.

But Holly nodded, and accepted the red cup he handed her. She held it under the tap and let him fill it up. Annie was glad about that too – she'd heard about boys slipping drugs into girls' drinks at parties. As long as she saw the beer coming out of the keg, she could be sure it wasn't tainted.

Holly raised her cup, then slugged back half of it in one gulp.

"Woah! This girl can party!" said Chad.

Holly beamed and finished the beer. When Chad offered her a refill, Annie expected Holly to decline. But Holly held out the cup and let him fill it up again.

"What are you doing?" Annie whispered frantically.

"Don't be such a baby," said Holly. "It's a party. When I get a buzz, I'll stop."

Annie was pretty sure that wasn't how it worked. She suspected that drunkenness sneaked up on a person – so it was more likely that Holly would be well past "buzzed" before she even realized it. Especially if she kept knocking back drinks in one gulp, like she had with that first one.

And the second.

And the third.

Chad kept pouring and Holly kept drinking.

And Annie kept panicking.

"Sure you don't want one?" Chad asked, offering Annie an empty cup.

"No thanks," said Annie, firmly. "And I think Holly should slow down."

Chad rolled his eyes. "Whatever." Then he grabbed Holly's hand and pulled her onto the dance floor, leaving Annie by the keg to stare after them.

"Hey, there, Econ!" came a familiar voice in her ear. "Wanna dance?"

Annie didn't. Not even a little bit. On the other hand, she'd be better able to keep an eye on Holly if she was on the dance floor too, so she forced a smile and followed Todd into the mass of writhing bodies.

He immediately pulled her close, and began swaying to the music. She could smell alcohol on his breath and he was sweating more than Annie did after a bout.

Gross.

Holly and Chad were grinding together now. Annie was sure Holly wouldn't be rubbing herself against a stranger if she hadn't drank so much, so fast.

Annie nearly jumped out of her skin when Todd suddenly pressed his hips to hers and began to rotate them, mimicking Chad and Holly's movements.

"Stop that!" Annie hissed, pushing away from him.

"Jeez." Todd gave her a condescending look. "Uptight much?"

In the next second, Annie felt an ice-cold splash on the back of her neck.

She squealed and jumped, swivelling round to see that a girl in a micro-mini had just spilled an entire cup of beer down her back.

"Ohmygodohmygodohmygodsorrysorrysorry," the girl slurred. "That was totally an ax … ax…"

"An accident?" Annie supplied tersely.

"Yes. An ax-i-*dent*!" The girl let out a sloppy laugh, then stumbled off towards the keg to replace her spilled drink.

Annie turned to Todd, who seemed to be trying not to crack

up. "I'm going to dry off," she said, then pushed her way through the dancing couples in search of a towel.

After a few wrong turns she found the frat house kitchen. It was beyond grungy, but there was a roll of paper towels beside the mildewed sink. She gathered up a handful and awkwardly contorted herself as she tried to press them to the back of her shirt.

A girl with an undercut hairstyle and a Muse T-shirt came into the kitchen. "You look like you could use a hand," she said, chuckling.

Annie gratefully accepted her help. The girl soaked up the liquid from the back of Annie's shirt and tossed the wet paper towels in an overflowing bin.

"There. You don't look like a wet T-shirt contestant any more," she said with a grin. "I'm Sasha, by the way."

"I'm Annie. This is my first frat party," Annie admitted. "I think it might also be my last."

"Frat parties aren't really my thing either," Sasha said. "But I promised my friend Mark I'd stop by. Luckily there's always plenty of other cool stuff happening on campus." She gave Annie an appraising look. "Are you a foreign exchange student?"

"No," Annie said. "I'm from London originally but I live here now."

Sasha sighed enviously. "God, London sounds so cool. I want to do my junior abroad at a university in London."

Sasha asked Annie loads of questions about London, which Annie was only too happy to answer. She loved talking about the city she'd grown up in, especially to someone so bright and well-informed. Eventually the conversation turned to music. It turned out that they liked loads of the same bands.

"Hey," said Sasha, "I'm going to check out my friend's band at Ziggy's later. Want to come with?"

"I wish I could," Annie said. "But I'd better get back to my friend. We came here together."

Annie said goodbye to her new friend and made her way back to the dance floor. Not surprisingly, in her absence Todd had found himself another dance partner. That didn't bother her, but her stomach flipped over when she realized that Holly and Chad were nowhere to be seen.

Pushing down the swell of panic in her chest, she approached Todd and tapped him on the shoulder.

He turned his bleary eyes to her and gave her a silly grin. "Wanna dance?"

"No, I don't. I want to find my friend."

"Oh … you mean the little redheaded hottie who was mackin' it with Chad?"

Annie frowned. "Yeah. Her."

Todd drunkenly nuzzled his dance partner's ear, then turned back to Annie. "He probably took her upstairs. Knowing Chad, they're gonna be a while." He waggled his eyebrows at her suggestively.

Annie felt a chill run up her spine. This was not good. Even if Holly had been sober, heading upstairs in a frat house with a boy she barely knew would be a bad idea! The fact that she was wasted made it exponentially worse. A thousand horror stories ran through Annie's mind.

She shoved Todd out of her way and shouldered through the crowd once again, this time heading for the stairs that led to the fraternity brothers' bedrooms.

It was the last place in the world she wanted to go.

But it was the only place she needed to be.

Heart racing, Annie made her way up the stairs. Girls snapped at her, assuming she was skipping the queue for the toilet. She ignored them and kept climbing. On the second floor, she found a long hallway of doors – all of them closed!

Damn, she thought. *Am I going to have to knock on all of them?* She was furious with Holly even as she feared for her friend's safety. She knew "Holly Terror" liked to act as though she were a lot more sophisticated than most girls their age, but Annie suspected that underneath the facade she was probably just as naive as the rest of them.

Drunk and alone in a dark room with a frat boy, Holly would be just as vulnerable as Annie herself would be.

She pressed her ear to the first door and heard heavy breathing and the squeaking of bed springs.

"I'm going to be sick," Annie whispered to herself. She was about to pound on the door when heard a muffled voice calling out the name Emily from the other side.

Annie hurried down the hall to the next door. She mustered her courage and knocked. Two seconds later, a scowling boy flung the door open.

"What?" he demanded. He pulled foam ear plugs out of his ears.

"I-I'm sorry. I was looking for Holly."

"Holly?" The boy's eyes flashed with irritation. "I don't know anyone named Holly. And if you don't mind, I'm trying to study here, because I have a physics exam on Monday morning!" He slammed the door in her face.

Annie moved to the next door, unsure what to do.

Luckily, at that moment, a boy came out of the bathroom. He had a friendly, open face and wore an Omega Alpha T-shirt.

Annie approached him. "Excuse me…"

"Hi," he said. "You lost?"

More than you know, Annie thought. She took a deep breath. "Can you tell me which room is Chad's?"

The boy frowned, momentarily confused. "Chad Davis? Or Chad Bartonelli?" He scratched his chin.

Annie had no idea. Desperately, she tried to recall if he'd ever told them his last name.

"He plays soccer," said Annie, remembering the jacket he'd had on at the café.

"Davis," the boy concluded. "Shoulda' known. Third door on the left." He gave her a worried look. "Are you sure you want to be up here?"

Ignoring his concerns, Annie ran down the hall, not stopping until she reached Chad's room.

"Holly!" she shouted, banging on the door with her fist. "Holly, are you in there?"

Nothing.

Annie knocked again, even harder. "Holly?"

The door swung open, and there was Chad, bare-chested, leaning with one hand on the door frame. He smiled at her. "If you're looking for Little Miss Jail Bait, she's not here."

Annie blinked, not sure if she should believe him. After all, he probably wouldn't admit to having an underage girl in his room. "Would you mind if I came in and checked?"

Chad's smile went icy. "Yeah. As a matter of fact, I would mind."

That was when Annie heard a sound behind him – it was the sound of sheets rustling.

Holly *was* in there.

"Let me in," she demanded.

Chad shook his head, stretching his other arm out to the opposite side of the door frame, barring her way. "I'm busy," he said.

Annie's chest tightened; her mind whirled.

And suddenly a word flashed in her head: *juke!*

She stepped forward, to Chad's right. Instinctively, he leaned to block her path, but in one swift movement, Annie dodged to the left, ducking under his arm and into the shadowy room.

"Holly!" she cried to the figure sprawled on the bed.

"It's Ashley," said the girl, sitting up to glare at Annie. "And I don't know who you are, or who Holly is. So if you don't mind, get lost."

Annie could only gape. She turned to Chad, who was still

lounging in the doorway.

"Last I saw, Holly was with you on the dance floor," she said firmly. "Please, tell me where she went."

Chad sighed, clearly bored with the whole episode. "While we were dancing she let it slip that she was only sixteen. I may be buzzed, but I'm not stupid. No girl's worth getting arrested for, not even one as cute as your friend."

It was all Annie could do to keep from slapping him across the face. Or better yet, kicking him in the groin.

"So where is she?" she demanded.

"Check the front lawn," Chad said. "She looked like she was gonna puke, so I walked her to the front door and told her to go outside and barf in the snow." He shrugged. "Then I met up with Ashley, and I kind of lost track of your friend after that."

Annie didn't waste another minute. She bounded out of the room, down the stairs, and outside.

"Holly!" she called. "Holly, are you out here?"

There was moment of pure panic before she heard the low groaning coming from behind a tree. She hurried through the snow in the direction of the sound.

Holly was huddled in a ball at the base of the tree trunk, shaking uncontrollably, half of her face resting in a pool of vomit.

"Oh god." Annie's knees buckled first with relief, then with fear. "Oh god! Holly!"

Holly lifted her face to look at Annie, but her eyes rolled back in her head. Her stomach heaved and Annie watched in horror as she threw up again.

The sound and the smell were atrocious, but Annie somehow managed to hold down her own supper. She dropped to her knees and stroked her friend's back.

"Holly, we've got to get you back to the dorm."

"OK," said Holly, her voice hollow and small. She lifted her head again and attempted to stand, but her legs crumpled beneath her.

Again, she vomited – even more violently than before. When she was finished, she lay still and silent.

Annie nudged her. "Holly?"

No response.

"Holly?"

Still, no reaction. Annie had never felt so helpless in her life. This time she shook Holly hard.

Nothing!

Hands trembling, Annie dug in her pocket for her phone. A tear rolled down her cheek, landing on the touch screen. Her fingers quivered, both from the cold and fear.

What should I do? She didn't really know. Annie's whole brain felt numb.

Somewhere in the back of her mind, she knew she should call Holly's mother. But Holly's mum was too far away to be of immediate assistance. Telling her that her sixteen-year-old daughter was passed out in the snow outside a frat house would only cause the woman to panic. At the moment, Annie simply didn't have the strength to deal with anyone's hysteria but her own, which was bubbling inside her now like a volcano, ready to erupt.

Maybe she could run back to the dorm to get one of the coaches, but she couldn't bear the thought of leaving Holly here all alone.

She didn't even know if Holly was still breathing. *Oh god, Holly, please, please be breathing!*

Annie couldn't think straight. Even the most basic emergency procedures seemed to evade her. Her head spun.

"Pull yourself together, Annie," she told herself, shaking her head vigorously. "Your teammate needs you."

As if on autopilot, her finger pressed buttons on her phone. The phone chirped softly and then it was ringing. Annie pressed the phone to her ear.

As calmly as she could, she told the emergency services operator what the problem was, and where the paramedics could find them.

The operator told her to check to see if Holly was breathing.

Yes, thank god, she was.

She stayed on with the operator until she could hear the sirens approaching. When the ambulance came speeding up in front of the frat house, the snow glowed red and blue in the flashing lights.

She told the EMTs exactly what had happened. That Holly had had a lot to drink, in a very short time.

"Has she taken any drugs?"

Not that Annie was aware of.

"Could someone have slipped her something?"

Maybe. Annie hadn't been watching Holly the whole time. So, yes, anything was possible.

Annie's tears were flowing freely now. She didn't even bother to brush them away.

She was suddenly overcome with a wave of guilt. She should have insisted Holly stop drinking, or threatened to report her to the coaches. She should have stayed with her the whole time, instead of talking to Sasha for so long...

Annie was aware of the party-goers looking on as the paramedics loaded Holly onto a stretcher and into the ambulance. Annie climbed in beside her, wondering vaguely where that jerk Chad was right now.

This was all his fault, after all.

But, no. It wasn't his fault any more than it was Annie's. He'd contributed to the situation, certainly. But this was Holly's fault. She'd made terrible choices tonight.

And now she was unconscious, on her way to the hospital.

Annie heard the siren wail as the ambulance sped off into the night. She felt as though she were in some kind of toxic fog as she called Sue, told her the whole miserable tale, and asked her to relay it all to Cherry Bomb.

Exiting the campus in the speeding emergency vehicle, Annie peered out of the small square window in the rear door.

As she watched Fraternity Row growing smaller in the distance, she could see that the Omega Alpha party was still going on.

An underage girl was being driven away in an ambulance, but

no one seemed to care. Students were still dancing and drinking. The ambulance's arrival hadn't even put a dent in the festivities for five minutes.

Even though she hadn't had so much as a sip of alcohol, Annie felt sick to her stomach. Suddenly, all she wanted was to go home.

Chapter Seventeen

Annie spent the rest of the night in a hard plastic chair at Holly's bedside.

She may have dozed, but she never really slept. When she did manage to close her eyes for more than ten minutes, she was assaulted with terrible images:

Todd pressing himself against her as though he had a right to.

The girl in Chad's bed who wasn't Holly.

Holly, face down in her own vomit.

Blue and red lights in the snow.

The doctor telling Annie and Cherry Bomb that Holly was having her stomach pumped.

Holly, looking pale and fragile, when they finally rolled her into the hospital room on a trolley.

At five in the morning, Annie gave up trying to sleep. She tiptoed out of the hospital room into the dimly lit corridor and took her phone out of her pocket. Scrolling down her contacts, she phoned Dad.

She knew he'd be awake, probably already in the shop, baking fresh muffins for the day ahead. He picked up on the second ring.

"Annie?" Dad's voice was tight with panic. "Annie, what is it?"

"I'm all right," she assured him quickly. "I'm fine."

"Nobody calls at five in the morning to say they're fine," he said, still sounding frightened. "Tell me what's wrong."

"It's not me, it's Holly," she began, leaning against the cold wall. "See, there was this party…"

The story came out in a long rush, and Dad listened as she explained to him every last detail of the worst night of her life.

"I'm sorry, Dad," she finished finally. "I knew it was wrong to go to the party. We should have never been there."

"Damn right you shouldn't have been," her father agreed, but his tone was more relieved than angry. He rarely cursed, which told Annie how much her story had upset him.

"I really am sorry." She let out a long sigh. "I just want to come home."

"I'll be there by ten," Dad promised. "And you can expect a long lecture about all this on the way home."

"I guessed as much," Annie grumbled. But she knew she deserved it.

Because as bad as things were, she understood that they could have been worse.

Much worse.

She went back into Holly's room and was surprised to find her awake.

"I'm not dreaming?" she asked in a croaky voice.

Annie shook her head. "Nope."

Holly pressed her lips together as her eyes flickered to the IV tube in her arm, then to the monitor, pulsing with coloured lights in the shadowy room. Her eyes glistened with tears that spilled over onto her cheeks. "How could I have been so stupid?"

Annie had no answer. She could only shrug.

"I'm such a jerk! I should have listened to you. I just wanted to have a wild, crazy time, something to talk about when we got home."

Annie allowed a tiny grin. "Well, you definitely accomplished that."

Holly laughed, but it ended in a sob. "I'm so sorry," she said. "I'm sorry for forcing you to go to that stupid party, and for putting you through this."

"I know," said Annie.

Holly put her hand to her forehead and winced. Annie could only imagine the headache Holly was experiencing at the moment. Maybe a hangover was nature's way of reminding you to be more careful in the future.

"How can I ever thank you for sticking by me?" said Holly softly, her bottom lip trembling.

"You don't have to," said Annie. "I'm your friend. You would have done the same for me."

"I wouldn't have had to. You wouldn't have been idiotic enough to get yourself into that situation in the first place." Holly broke into a fresh burst of tears. This time they came in deep, shuddering sobs.

Annie held her hand and let her cry. She understood that Holly was filled with more feelings than she could process at one time – regret, guilt, humiliation.

When Holly was finally calm again, Annie took a tissue from the bedside table and wiped her cheeks. "Promise me you'll never do anything like that again," she whispered.

"I swear."

"OK, then."

Annie grinned and sunk back down into the hard plastic chair. "And for the record, this wasn't exactly what I had in mind when I said I wanted to be your roommate."

Holly laughed weakly. "Yeah, well, my derby name is Holly Terror for a good reason."

They fell into a companionable silence, each lost in her own thoughts.

After a few minutes, Annie heard the sound of slow, deep breathing that meant Holly had drifted back to sleep.

She closed her own eyes, the exhaustion overtaking her.

But this time she didn't conjure up any unpleasant visions of sweaty dancers or hospital trolleys.

She couldn't wait to crawl into her own bed. She wanted to be home right that instant. But weirdly, when she thought of home, the first image that popped into her head was Jesse's face. She pictured him pushing his black hair out of his intense blue eyes and greeting her with his wide, slow smile.

At long last, she slept.

"Hey, you party animals…"

Annie opened her eyes slowly and saw Luna and Sue smiling down at her. The room was now filled with bright winter sunlight and it took her a moment to remember where she was. When she did, she turned quickly in the direction of Holly's bed to see if she was still in one piece.

She was … and she was smiling awkwardly at her visitors. "I bet you guys think I'm a total screw-up, huh?"

"Ten different kinds of stupid," said Luna cheerfully, popping herself onto the edge of Holly's bed. "But nobody's perfect."

"I'm going to assume you learned your lesson," said Sue, leaning down to place a loud kiss on Holly's forehead.

"You bet I did."

"How are you doing, Annie?" Sue asked, handing her a tall cardboard cup of hot tea.

"Tired," Annie said, yawning.

"Well, I hear being a hero can take a lot out of you," Luna observed.

Annie blushed. "I'm not a hero."

"I disagree," said Holly. Her voice was still raspy from the tube that had been down her throat when the doctors pumped her stomach.

Annie took a long, grateful sip of her tea. "So how much trouble are we in?"

Luna and Sue exchanged glances.

"Mad Donna drove us over," Luna explained. "She and Cherry Bomb are down the hall, handling the discharge papers. On the way here, Mad Donna was talking to the camp director on the phone."

"And…" Annie prompted.

Luna shrugged. "The bad news is, they're all pretty angry."

"But the good news," Sue added quickly, "is they're going to let you off with just a strong reprimand. Camp's over, so what else could they do? Except…"

Sue trailed off, clearing her throat.

"Except what?" Annie prompted.

"Well," said Luna, with a frown, "let's just say there's no point in signing up for next year's camp. Because neither of you will be allowed back."

Annie's cheeks burned. The idea of being banned from boot camp – or anywhere else for that matter – was very upsetting. But then again, it could have been much worse.

"I think the coaches figure they're partly responsible for not keeping close enough tabs on us," Sue continued. "If they make a big deal about it, other parents might find out and complain about insufficient supervision and stricter rules and junk like that."

"When we left them at the nurse's station, they were grumbling something about not letting one bad apple spoil it for the bunch."

Holly grimaced. For a girl who liked to be seen as tough, Annie was beginning to understand that Holly Terror wasn't all that happy about being thought of as "bad".

Luna improved the mood in the room by withdrawing a pair of rainbow-striped skate laces from her pocket. "These are from Sue and me," she said, handing the colourful laces to Holly. "A little get-well gift."

"Thanks," said Holly.

"Yeah," said Sue, sheepishly. "We figured it would soften the blow…"

The next thing Annie knew, Holly's mother was thundering into the room.

The first thing she did was throw her arms around her daughter and hug her for a good two minutes, crying softly and murmuring how much she loved Holly.

Then she got down to business.

"What were you thinking?" she demanded, her face flushed with anger, her voice sombre.

Holly looked down at her hands. "I know. I'm sorry."

"You're grounded for the foreseeable future, young lady."

Annie was incredibly uncomfortable. This conversation really should have been taking place in private. In Holly's mother's defence, though, she was so upset Annie suspected she hadn't even registered the fact there was anyone else in the room.

Now Holly's mother took a deep breath and delivered the

final verdict. "I hate to do this to you, Holly, but I feel I don't have a choice — you won't be trying out for the All-Star team."

Holly's mouth dropped open and her face went white. "Mom! No!"

"I'm sorry, Holly, but you need to learn your lesson."

Annie's heart broke for Holly. She wanted to point out that a stomach pump and a hangover from hell would surely be enough of a lesson for anyone. Taking away roller derby, the thing Holly loved most, seemed so extreme.

It was hard for Annie to understand Holly's mother's reaction. Back in the UK, attitudes were more relaxed. The drinking age was eighteen, and teenagers as young as sixteen could drink alcohol with a meal at the pub. Lots of Annie's friends had been allowed to drink at home. Annie had never really tried alcohol, because she'd always been a serious athlete — she'd never wanted her gymnastics performance to suffer. For the same reason now, she wasn't interested in drinking because roller derby was too important to her.

A feeling of dread began to creep up Annie's spine as it occurred to her that maybe Dad would hand down the same punishment to her. If he did, she knew she would be just as devastated as Holly was — maybe even more.

"The coaches are waiting for me to sign some paperwork at the nurses' station," her mother said. "They've brought along your skate bag and your luggage, so we'll be leaving for home from here."

Holly nodded.

Then her mum was out of the door, and stomping down the hall.

"Well, that sucks," said Luna, sighing.

"God, what's the big deal," said Sue. "It's not like you're the first teenager who's ever had a drink."

"Tell me about it." Holly leaned against the pillow and closed her eyes.

"We should probably get going," said Sue. "The coaches want to leave as soon as they hand over your bags to your mom. Annie, they told us to tell you to come back to campus with us."

Annie felt a knot of dread in her stomach. This really was goodbye. She'd be seeing Holly again, of course – well, not on the roller derby track any time soon, but at least they could hang out at school. And if her plan to set Sue up with Lauren worked out, she might be seeing her occasionally, too. But Luna was from New Jersey – not exactly a day trip.

The girls hugged, and made plans to email and Skype regularly.

Then Sue, Luna, and Annie headed for the door.

"Annie!" Holly called.

Annie leaned back into the room, and her heart broke to see the expression of loss on her friend's face.

Holly waved her over to the bed. "You've got to make the All-Star team," she said, her voice tight with tears. "You've got to." Then, to Annie's surprise, she held out the rainbow skate laces and pressed them into Annie's hand. "Do it for me."

Annie nodded, fighting back tears of her own. "I'll do my

best," she promised.

Then she tucked the laces into her pocket and hurried down the hallway after the others.

An hour later, Dad's truck was pulling up to the curb in front of the student centre. Annie sprang up from where she'd been sitting on the top step and ran to greet him, marvelling over the fact that it had been a mere seven days ago that Jesse had dropped her off in that very spot.

Suddenly, it felt like a lifetime.

Dad caught her in a hug and squeezed. "I'm glad you're all right."

"Me too."

Then he helped her settle her bags in the back of the truck and they were off.

Annie was aware that something was different, but it took her a moment to realize what it was.

"The fan belt isn't screeching any more," she said, surprised.

"Your pal Jesse's mechanic friend fixed it for me. Good as new, now."

"Cool," said Annie, but she frowned. *Your pal Jesse.* For some reason she wasn't exactly thrilled by the sound of that.

"So…" said Dad. "I suppose you don't need me to tell you what a dangerous stunt you pulled."

Annie shook her head.

"You broke the camp rules, and you put yourself in a very bad situation."

"Guilty as charged," sighed Annie.

"On the upside, you were smart enough not to drink. You know it's against the law in this country. We live here now, and it's important that we stick to the rules. If you *are* going to drink, Beanie, I want you to promise me you're going to do it somewhere safe, around people you trust."

Annie gave her dad a smile. "I promise."

Dad lifted one eyebrow. "Cross your heart?"

Annie nodded her head emphatically and put her hands over her chest. "Cross my heart, hope to die, stick a needle in my eye."

"Well you don't need to go that far," said Dad with a smile. "Lecture over."

Annie was glad. All she wanted to do was put the horrible night behind her.

Her eyes fell on the pile of CDs she'd left in the truck the week before, when she'd expected to be riding to Great Lakes University in Dad's pickup.

Music, she decided. Music would help get the whole ugly incident out of her mind. She shuffled through the bunch and smiled when she found the homemade CD, the one that had been left in the postbox on Valentine's Day by a so-called secret admirer.

AKA Dad.

Only now did Annie realize that she'd never bothered playing it.

Slipping it out of the sleeve on which her "admirer" had boldly printed "YOU ROCK", Annie pressed the disc into the truck's CD player.

Seconds later, the dreamy rasp of Elvis Costello's voice filled the cab, as he sang his moody rendition of "My Funny Valentine".

"Great song," said Annie.

"Who is it by?" asked Dad.

Annie rolled her eyes. "Duh. You should know. You're the one who—" She stopped short because she suddenly realized that Dad really *didn't* know who was singing the little love song. Dad had never been a big fan of Elvis Costello.

In fact, as far as Annie knew, her father didn't own a single Elvis Costello album. Which meant that he probably didn't burn this CD.

Heart thudding, she popped the CD out of the player and, for the first time, looked at the playlist on the face of the disc.

Punk rock love songs, one and all.

"Dad," said Annie, "you really didn't send this to me, did you?"

Dad shook his head. "I guess the mystery remains."

"Maybe," said Annie, feeling the corners of her mouth turning upward. *And maybe not.* She couldn't be sure, but she had a very strong hunch.

Now Dad reached into the console between the seats and pulled out a white paper bag which Annie recognized immediately.

It was a Rosie Lee's bag. And inside were half a dozen shortbread cookies with green shamrocks iced on top.

"Gotta be ready for St Paddy's day," Dad said, grinning.

Annie took a cookie out of the bag and bit into it gratefully. It was sweet and crisp and wonderful.

Only now did she realize how much she'd missed the taste of Dad's baking.

Annie closed her eyes and took another bite, savouring the flavour. It tasted buttery and sweet, but there was something better. Something more.

It tasted like home.

Chapter Eighteen

On Monday morning, Annie arrived at her locker to find a swarm of people waiting for her.

This time, though, it wasn't because there was some nasty message on her locker.

This time, they wanted information.

And since Holly was still at home recovering, the revealing of said information fell to the only other Liberty Heights High student who had been there.

"What the heck happened to you guys at that camp?" Carmen asked in amazement. "I heard Holly tried to commit suicide and ended up in the hospital."

"I heard you both got arrested," said Liz.

"That's ridiculous," said Annie, opening her locker and

shoving her jacket inside. "Holly absolutely did *not* attempt suicide, and I'm very happy to report that neither of us has a police record."

Lauren shook her head, confused. "So what *did* happen? Is Holly OK? Are you?"

"We're both fine," Annie assured her. "We just exercised a little bad judgment." She corrected herself. "OK, a *lot* of bad judgment." Annie sighed. "Well, I'd rather you heard the real story from me than believing these stupid rumours."

As she headed for her homeroom class, the girls fell into step beside her and Annie told them the whole story, beginning with meeting the boys at Ziggy's and ending with Holly's stomach being pumped at the hospital.

Her friends could hardly believe what they were hearing. They were especially taken aback by the news of Holly's punishment.

"No roller derby?" Sharmila gasped.

Annie sighed. "Not until next season."

"She must be devastated."

"That's the suckiest thing I've ever heard in my life!" said Carmen.

When the older girls headed off to their own homerooms, Lauren hung back. She looked more than a little worried.

"I can't believe Holly blew her chances of being on the All-Star team," she said heavily. "Out of all of us, she was the one who had a lock on it."

"I wouldn't say she blew it," said Annie. "I mean, it certainly wasn't as if she got super-drunk on purpose. She just got herself into a situation she couldn't handle."

"But she's going to be OK, right?" Lauren pressed. "It'll all come out fine?"

"Yes," Annie promised. Then she remembered something and gave Lauren a big smile. "Speaking of 'coming out fine', how did your week go? How did your family react to your big revelation?"

Lauren's expression changed from worry to joy. "I was so freaked out about telling them, but it was absolutely fine. My parents were super-supportive. My brother, too. Even my grandparents were understanding about it, just worried that other kids would be mean and intolerant."

Annie giggled. "Sounds like you've got some pretty hip grandparents."

"Yeah." Lauren laughed. "I guess I do. Ya know, I kind of got the feeling no one in my family was all that surprised. I mean, they've known me my whole life. Maybe they started to get the hint when I was the only sixth grade girl in America who didn't have a poster of the Jonas Brothers over my bed."

Annie smiled. "Or maybe they just love you to death, and they understood who the real Lauren was even before you realized it yourself."

Lauren nodded, her eyes shining. "Yeah, maybe. In any case, I'm out, and I'm happy."

"Well then," said Annie, draping an arm over Lauren's shoulder, "let me tell you about this girl I met at camp…"

* * *

Later, Annie walked into her English class to find Kelsey perched on Tyler's desk. It was strange, but after everything she'd been through, something as silly as being jealous over an ex-boyfriend seemed too pointless to get upset about.

Tessa, who played for the Derby Dolls, smiled at her when she sat down. "Don't worry. I'm not going to ask a single question. I just got all the deets from Carmen in the bathroom. I'm just glad you guys are all right."

"Thanks," said Annie.

"Hey, Annie," said Kelsey in a disdainful tone. "Heard you got into trouble last week. What happened? Did you try to hook up with some hunky frat guy who was out of your league?"

Annie just rolled her eyes.

"I also heard Holly practically OD'ed on drugs or something."

Again, Annie gritted her teach, refusing to rise to the bait.

Kelsey let out a cruel little giggle. "I always knew you roller girls were trash."

"I guess we can't all be as sweet and innocent as you cheerleaders are," Annie said, her voice dripping with sarcasm.

The entire classroom burst into laughter, just as Ms Schwartz entered the room.

"I'm glad to see you're all in such a jovial mood today," the teacher said. "Could it have anything to do the fact that we're finishing up our study of *Sense and Sensibility*?"

As she listened to Ms Schwartz discuss the romantic trials

and tribulations of Marianne Dashwood, Annie started thinking about her own situation. Like Miss Dashwood, Annie had fallen for a handsome, charismatic man, only to discover he had the soul and character of a scumbag. But throughout her heartbreak and disappointment, Marianne could always count on her steady and honourable friend, Colonel Brandon.

Just like Annie could always count on Jesse.

The realization hit Annie like a block from Dee Stroyer. Funny, cute, and cool Jesse was her Colonel Brandon! He was the boy she should have set her sights on from the start. He was the boy she should have liked all along.

Maybe, she thought, *somewhere deep down, she always had.*

But what should she do about it now?

Annie was pretty sure Jesse was her secret admirer. But asking him outright would be off-the-charts awkward – especially since she'd mistakenly thought the CD was from her dad and told Jesse as much.

She'd just have to look for a sign that he was still interested, and wait for the right moment to tell him how she felt.

She just hoped she hadn't left it too long.

"Wait up, Annie!"

Annie was just opening the door to Rosie Lee's when she heard Lexie's voice behind her.

"Lexie!" Annie threw her arms around her friend. "I was so

disappointed when you weren't in school today. Aren't you sick?"

"Nah!" Lexie — ever the quirky dresser — was decked out in a tailored tuxedo jacket with long tails that flopped down over a pair of tattered blue jeans. On her head she wore a vintage silk top hat with a fat satin rose pinned to the brim. "I was up all night working on a painting. It was like I was possessed or something! I just couldn't stop painting! I didn't crawl into bed until six this morning, so my mom let me stay home and sleep."

Annie laughed. "Well, you missed a lot of excitement."

Lexie tipped her hat and grinned. "How about I help you out behind the counter while you fill me in."

"I'd love that," said Annie sincerely. "But you worked here all week. Aren't you sick of this place?"

"Not at all," said Lexie. "In fact, I loved it. And now I'm even more addicted to your dad's cinnamon scones."

The girls swept into the shop, giggling, only to find Dad once again displaying a newspaper, his face beaming with pride.

"Don't tell me they ran the Queen of Tarts ad again," groaned Annie.

"Better!" said Dad. "We've made the Dining Out section of the *Gazette*. The food critic came in last week to sample our menu. It's our first review!"

"From the way you're smiling," said Lexie, "I think we can conclude it's a good one."

Dad handed the paper to Annie, who took it eagerly.

"'Delicious baked goods...'" she murmured, scanning the article. "'Delightful coffees ... cosy atmosphere...'" she gasped.

"Oh my god!"

"What?" asked Lexie. "Oh my god what?"

Annie pointed to the last paragraph. "Read this!"

Lexie took the paper, her eyes darting over the words. "'One of the most endearing aspects of Rosie Lee's,'" she read aloud, "'is the staff. The server who assisted me during my visit was charming and friendly. In fact, she insisted I sample the cinnamon scones, which were incredible. However, when I asked her to box up a few more to bring home, she admitted that she herself had just eaten the last one!'"

Dad and Annie laughed so hard they nearly cried.

"You know what they say," said Lexi, beaming. "Always leave 'em wanting more!"

"Right!" said Dad. "Lexie, how can I ever thank you?"

"A cinnamon scone would be good."

As Dad disappeared into the kitchen to grab a warm one from the oven, Annie and Lexie hurried into aprons. Thanks to the review, the place was packed. Mothers were bringing little children in for afternoon snacks and local professionals were popping in on their coffee breaks. A book club was seated at a table by the window.

Annie couldn't be happier. Dad had wanted Rosie Lee's to become a popular gathering place, and now it seemed his dream was coming true.

And maybe, if she could only get up the nerve to tell Jesse how she felt about him, hers would too.

Chapter Nineteen

The next afternoon, Annie arrived at the rink, her skate bag slung over her shoulder, her stomach fluttering with butterflies.

It was the day of the All-Star team try-outs.

The first face she saw was Lauren's, looking even more nervous than Annie felt. As Lauren approached her, Annie shot a quick glance in the direction of the rental booth.

Jesse was nowhere to be seen.

"Can you believe how many girls are here?" Lauren asked when she reached Annie. "Coach Ritter did a rough count and said there were close to forty. And there's still time for more to show up."

"Well, look at it this way," said Annie, putting an optimistic spin on the situation, "the more girls there are, the better the chances she'll put together a really awesome team."

"And the more likely we won't be a part of it," Lauren grumbled.

Annie gave her a playful nudge. "Attitude counts! You have to think positively."

"Easy for you to say," Lauren countered. "You've just spent seven days skating with some of the best coaches around."

Annie had to admit, she was hoping her newfound skills would make her look good in front of Coach Ritter. She was nervous but at the same time confident that she had as good a chance as anyone else to make the team – and, thanks to boot camp, in some cases, better.

She dashed off to the locker room, which was teeming with girls from the whole league. Nearly all of the Derby Dolls had turned up to try out, a good number of High Rollers were in attendance, and a few Prairie Girls as well.

Annie had chosen a tough-looking outfit for the try-outs. She was wearing her favourite cobalt-blue hot pants, a black ribbed cotton tank top with a skull and crossbones graphic on the front, and a pair of black fishnet tights. She'd gone extra-heavy on the black eyeliner and outlined her lips with dark red liner. The only whimsical touch to her look were Holly's get-well rainbow laces.

"I'm thinking of you, Holl," she whispered as she laced up her skates. "This is for both of us!"

When she got out on the track, many of the girls were already warming up, skating laps, or stretching on the musty old carpet. As she joined the skaters she was delighted to find that she had her very own cheering section!

Lexie was front and centre, hooting and hollering, along with Annie's teammates Carmen, Liz, and Sharmila. They waved and called her name and Lauren's, wishing them both luck.

Annie felt a tug of sadness knowing that even if she did make the travel team, not all of the Liberty Belles would be a part of it, as their schedules prevented them from committing to an entire summer of practice and out-of-town bouts. It would only be herself and Lauren representing the Belles today and she wanted more than anything for them both to make the team.

Annie slammed around the track, aware that she had more stamina than ever after the gruelling week of camp. Her muscles pulsed with power and her moves were smoother than before.

On her second lap, she glanced towards her "fan club", and felt her heart thud when she realized that another member had joined their ranks.

Standing beside Lexie was Jesse! And he was holding a hand-lettered sign above his head:

YOU ROCK, ANNE R KEY!

Annie was so delighted by the sign that she nearly collided with the girl in front of her.

"Watch it!" the girl growled.

Annie ignored her, her eyes lingering for a moment on Jesse's, then moving up to admire the banner. He'd obviously gone to some trouble to make it – the message handwritten boldly and neatly on neon green card.

She'd seen the writing before, she was certain. It was exactly the same writing that had been on the mysterious Valentine's Day card.

Even the message was the same: *You rock.*

This was what she'd been waiting for! *A sign.* Literally!

It was all she could do to keep from leaping off the track and running straight into his arms. Jesse was her most loyal supporter, her secret admirer, her valentine!

Her thoughts were interrupted by the sound of Coach Ritter's whistle. The All-Star hopefuls gathered at the side of the track.

"Time to begin," Coach announced. "We'll kick things off with a speed and endurance test. The goal is to skate twenty-five laps in under five minutes."

A groan rose up from the group. Annie, however, allowed herself a tiny grin. She'd been skating at full tilt for seven straight days – her endurance was better than it had ever been.

Coach broke the girls into groups of ten for this test. Annie and Lauren would both skate in the fourth batch. It was nerve-racking, waiting for the first groups to take their turns. Dee Stroyer was part of the first bunch, and it was slightly disheartening for Annie to see the bully win her heat with a time of four minutes and thirty-nine seconds.

When it was Annie's turn, she breezed through the test in four minutes and twelve seconds, beating everyone in her group by several seconds. As she finished her twenty-fifth lap, her cheering section erupted in applause. She was pretty out of breath, and there was a slight stitch in her side, which she massaged gently as she watched the rest of her competitors finish the test. When Lauren, who was never one of the speediest skaters on the Liberty Belles, managed to squeak in at just under five minutes, Annie and the other Liberty Belles sent up a cheer. Lauren skated over to her and they high-fived gleefully.

The next test was designed to evaluate their blocking abilities, followed by another in which Coach would examine the level of their footwork. Annie was slightly disheartened to see that many of the girls excelled in both these areas. Still, she did her best. As she executed her moves, she could hear Mad Donna's and Cherry Bomb's voices in her head, shouting out tips and corrections. She obeyed these invisible coaches and ended up doing a fabulous job.

Then Coach Ritter gave them a break, telling them to drink water and stretch out if they needed to. While the girls enjoyed this brief rest period, Coach Ritter explained her philosophy for the All-Star programme.

"The main difference," she told them, twirling her whistle on its string, "will be that as an All-Star squad, we're going to use game strategies that are far more advanced than any we use during the regular season. On this elite All-Star team, you'll be expected to keep your head in the game and always find ways to put your particular talents to use. To that end, I'm going to teach you a drill called Kill Box."

"*Kill* Box?" Lauren echoed. "I don't think I like the sound of that."

Annie giggled. "It's probably not so bad. Sounds like it's all about catching on quickly and thinking on your feet. You've always been good at that."

The girls were divided into groups of four, three of whom would be blockers. The fourth would be jammer.

"I need the blockers to stagger," Coach instructed. "Girls, you'll take turns being on the inside. The blocker at the back will hit the jammer when she tries to pass on the outside. That blocker will then move up and the next one will take her place."

"See?" said Annie, giving Lauren's shoulder an encouraging pat. "That doesn't sound so bad."

"Not to you," said Lauren. "You're a jammer!"

Annie laughed. "And what part of 'hit the jammer' sounds *good* to you?"

Now Lauren laughed too, and Annie was glad she'd been able to help her friend shake off her nerves.

As it turned out, "hit the jammer" was the least of Annie's troubles. Her group of four included herself, two Prairie Girls and none other than Dee Stroyer. Dee shot Annie a searing look that said she wasn't going to make this easy.

And she didn't. As they skated around the track, Dee and the other blockers did an excellent job of swapping places to keep Annie from getting past. Dee especially was formidable, successfully bootie-blocking Annie out of bounds.

Annie frowned, hopping back onto the track on her toe stops. They resumed the drill, and minutes later, Dee had once again blocked Annie, even more roughly than before.

"Maybe we can arrange for a little hospital visit for *you*," Dee taunted, "just like your boozy little friend!"

The animosity of the remark took Annie aback. Healthy rivalry was one thing, but Dee's comment had crossed the line. "That's not funny," Annie snarled, scrambling back to her feet. "Sending people to the hospital isn't part of the game."

"I've sent you there before," said Dee. "I can easily do it again." Annie had an angry flashback to her October trip to the emergency room with an ankle injury, courtesy of Dee. Then she found herself picturing her more recent hospital visit with Holly.

In her mind, she saw the doctors rushing Holly down the corridor on a trolley; she pictured her friend unconscious in the bed, and then waking up and crying. She remembered a forlorn Holly saying goodbye as Annie left the room with Sue and Luna.

In that moment, Annie glanced down at the brightly coloured laces in her skates.

"*You've got to make the All Star team*," Holly had said. "*Do it for me.*"

It was the only inspiration Annie needed. When she came up to the next blocker, Annie expertly faked going around on the outside, just as she'd slipped past that horrible Chad in the doorway of his bedroom. Then she quickly swivelled round to skate backwards around the inside.

I'm through!

Elated, she flew past the other two blockers.

Smiling, Coach Ritter nodded and gave her a thumbs up. Glowing with triumph, Annie scanned the sidelines. Her friends were screaming their heads off, and Jesse was waving his homemade sign over his head.

Feeling brave, Annie winked and blew him a kiss, then laughed out loud at the surprised look on his face.

If anyone rocked, it was Jesse.

Chapter Twenty

At last, Coach blew the whistle for the last time.

Try-outs were over.

Annie and Lauren, sweaty and exhausted, skated to the side of the rink and treated themselves to long, cool gulps from their water bottles.

Annie felt her chances of making the team were good, but truthfully, there were so many talented skaters here. And Coach could only choose twenty.

As she sat on the musty carpet with the other hopefuls, Annie had a flashback to the day she'd tried out for the Liberty Belles. She'd been such a newbie, then!

In many ways, she felt as though she was an entirely different person now. Her skills were much improved, and she had more confidence – both on and off the track. Best of all, she had found lots of really great friends in her fellow roller girls.

And one roller boy … a boy with amazing taste in music, and lips she was suddenly dying to kiss!

Her thoughts were interrupted by the sound of someone clearing her throat. Annie looked up and her mouth dropped open in surprise as she saw a petite figure, her red hair hidden under a baseball cap.

"Holly!"

A murmur of curiosity rippled through the group.

"Hi, everybody," said Holly. "Bet you didn't expect to see me here."

"Didn't particularly *want* to, either," Dee sneered.

To Annie's delight, one of the Derby Dolls shot Dee a look. "Nobody asked you."

Dee scowled, but dropped her gaze to the carpet and shut up.

"I wanted to watch you guys try out," Holly explained.

"I didn't see you," said Lauren.

"Yeah, well, I was kind of skulking in the shadows near the rental booth. Hiding in shame, basically."

Annie heard the tremor in her friend's voice. Her instinct was to leap up and throw her arms protectively around Holly, but something told her that she needed to make this stand on her own. Annie forced herself to sit still and listen.

"So, yeah…" Holly said with a shrug. "I know you've all heard about my thrilling adventure over vacation. And I know you've all been judging me and saying I acted like a complete idiot." She paused, her eyes scanning her silent audience. "Well, I just came here to tell you … that you're right."

Many of the girls exchanged looks.

"You're right," Holly repeated, then gave a grim laugh. "I bet you were expecting me to say something different, huh? Bet you thought I was gonna be all pissed off and demand that you quit dissing me and acting all tough, like I usually do. Well, as much as I'd like to do that I can't … because everything you're thinking and saying about me is absolutely correct."

"Wow," whispered one of the Prairie Girls to the High Roller beside her. "That takes guts."

"See," Holly continued, "I had this amazing chance to do something I love – to come out here and skate my best, and try to make this All-Star team. But instead, I was a loser. I risked my dignity just because I thought it would be cool to party hard." Now Holly's eyes darted to Annie, her expression filled with regret. "And I also dragged someone I really care about into my mess. So I just wanted to come by and remind you all how lucky you are, just to be here. As I was watching you, my muscles actually ached to be out there on that track. You all did an amazing job and I wish I could have been a part of it."

Now Annie did stand up and gave Holly a long hug.

"You were awesome out there, Anne R. Key," Holly said. "I'm really proud of you."

"Not as proud as I am of you." Annie whispered, her throat tight with emotion. "And you happen to be pretty awesome yourself."

"Well, thanks." Holly cocked her head and smiled. "Sooo …
does that mean I can have my skate laces back?"

Annie laughed, and a moment later, Coach Ritter appeared
with her clipboard. She nodded at Holly, who looked suddenly
terrified. But when Coach gave Holly a kind smile, Annie could
feel all the tension drain out of her friend.

We all make mistakes, Annie thought. *Coach understands that.*

Holly gave the group one last smile, then went off to join the
other spectators. As Annie watched her go, she was pleased to
see that Dad had shown up. He must have closed Rosie Lee's a
little early to be here in time to hear the results. He was standing
with Lexie and the others, bouncing eagerly on the balls of his
feet, looking nervous and excited. Annie had to laugh. His nerves
were probably only partly due to the anticipation of finding out
whether Annie made the team. The fact that he had yet another
date with Coach Ritter, immediately after the try-outs, was
probably another reason!

As Annie watched her cheering section wringing their hands
and biting their lips anxiously, it occurred to her that, with the
notable exception of Mum, all of the people that mattered most
to her in the world were here in this rink, rooting for her.

In that moment, she realized that even if she didn't make the
team, she was one of the luckiest girls on the planet.

Now Coach Ritter stood before the group and began her
closing speech.

"This hasn't been an easy choice," she said. "You all set
a very high standard here today and you can all be proud of

your efforts. And for those of you who don't make the team, there is always next year." She drew a deep breath and dropped her eyes to the clipboard in her hand. "Here are the twenty members of the All-Star team. I'll read the names alphabetically. Lauren Anderson."

Annie had her arms around Lauren practically before the last syllable was out of coach's mouth.

"You did it!" she whispered. "Congratulations."

"Thanks, Annie!"

As Coach went down the list, Annie held her breath. Why did T have to be so close to the end of the alphabet? Around her, girls were clapping and cheering and squealing with excitement, while others swiped away tears or hung their heads in disappointment.

"Jennifer Silverman," Coach read. "Dakota Taylor."

Annie closed her eyes and crossed her fingers.

"Annie Turner!"

Annie felt her body flood with joy. She'd made it!

"Wooooooo!" Lexie cried. "Thatta girl, Annie!"

"Anne R. Key!" Jesse shouted. "You rock!"

Annie could almost feel his words, his voice, settling into her heart.

"Annamaria Vincent," Coach read. "Deanna Williams."

"Who's Deanna Williams?" Lauren asked, just as Dee Stroyer leaped to her feet, pumping her fist in the air.

"There's your answer," said Annie glumly.

As the girls who'd made the team drew together to celebrate, Annie came to a decision. If she and her nemesis were going to be teammates, someone was going to have to make the first move towards peace. It was clearly going to have to be Annie. Maybe now that they'd proven themselves equal, Dee would get over herself and start being civil. If not out of any genuine respect for Annie, at least for the good of the All-Star squad. That was what any serious roller girl would do.

She put a smile on her face and skated over to Dee.

"I know we've had our issues before," she said, extending her hand. "But now that we're teammates I hope we can get along."

To Annie's shock, Dee ignored her hand, and unclipped her helmet. "I'm not here to make friends. I'm here to play derby."

Annie watched her skate away, weaving through her celebrating teammates without even pausing to offer anyone congratulations.

Her loss, Annie thought. *I've got plenty of other great teammates and amazing friends.*

And it was time to go and celebrate with them. But first she had some unfinished business to take care of…

Annie accepted hugs and high fives from Lexie, Carmen, Sharmila, and Liz.

"Come on," said Liz. "Let's go grab some ice cream. I bet you're starving."

"Sorry, girls," she said to her friends, "But there's something I need to do." Glancing over at Jesse, she gave the girls a wink.

"And I think you all know what it is!"

At that Lexie let out another loud "Wooo-hoo!" and Annie laughed.

She took Jesse by the sleeve and tugged him to a quiet corner of the rink, then turned to look him directly in the eye.

"You were incredible out there," he began, but Annie pressed her finger to his lips.

"Thank you for the CD," she said, her eyes locked on his. "At first, I never dreamed it was from you. Then, when I finally played it and heard Elvis Costello singing 'your looks are laughable … unphotographable' I started to think maybe it was you. But I wasn't completely sure until I saw the sign."

Jesse gave her a confused look. "You saw a sign? Like, from *God*?"

"No," Annie giggled. "Like from the *sidelines*." She pointed to the banner he was still holding. "*This* sign, silly. When I saw the writing, I knew for definite you were the one who sent me the CD."

Jesse laughed. "I've gotta admit, at first I was kind of mad that you never thanked me for the mix. But when I realized that you honestly believed it was from your dad, I thought it was kind of hilarious."

"I wish you'd told me," Annie said, stepping closer to him.

"Yeah, well – " Jesse's eyes sparkled – "that would have been a major breach of the Secret Admirer Code of Behaviour. Keeping things on the down-low is the most important part of the gig."

"I'm sorry I didn't work it out sooner. I guess you think I'm kind of an idiot."

"Actually, I think you're kind of amazing." He smiled. "And about those lyrics … it's a great song, but I hope you know that there's nothing even remotely 'laughable' or 'unphotographable' about your looks. You're a beautiful person, Annie Turner. Inside and out."

Annie felt a rush of warmth and she leaned her face nearer to his. "What about Anne R. Key? What kind of person is she?"

Jesse chuckled softly. "She's a badass roller girl." He kissed her softly on the tip of her nose. "And she's also pretty hot."

Annie sighed and put her arms around his neck, pulling him close.

"You're the one I've been looking for," she whispered. "And the funny thing is, you were right there under my nose the whole time. I'm sorry I didn't see it sooner."

Jesse gave her his crooked grin. "No worries. As long as you got there in the end. Besides, you were definitely worth the wait."

He reached out and gently touched the side of her face. Annie flinched.

"What's wrong?"

"Nothing," she sighed. "It's just that this is pretty much the most amazingly romantic moment of my life. I wish I wasn't such a sweaty mess."

Jesse laughed softly, and the sound sent a tingle up her spine.

"I think I can learn to deal with that kind of thing," he whispered, leaning close. "After all, I'm in love with a roller girl. So I'd better get used to it."

Then he kissed her. It was the kiss she'd been waiting for her whole life. It was warm and sweet and perfect. How could it be anything else?

Because Jesse was in love with a roller girl.

And there was no mistaking it − she was completely and totally head over heels in love with him!

ALL ABOUT
Roller Derby

RULES OF THE GAME

A roller derby game is called a bout. A bout usually lasts sixty minutes and is divided into two-minute jams. During a jam, each of the two teams have five players on the track, all skating in the same direction. The blockers and pivots form a tight pack. The two jammers start behind them and race to break through the pack. The first jammer through the pack is designated the lead jammer. However, no points can be scored until the jammer passes the pack for a second time. The jammer then scores a point for every opponent that she overtakes, provided she passes the player in bounds and without penalties. Both jammers may score points for the duration of the two-minute jam or until the lead jammer calls off the jam. A jammer typically scores four points every time she makes it through the pack. If she overtakes the other jammer she scores a fifth point, and this is known as a Grand Slam. The team with the most points at the end of the bout wins.

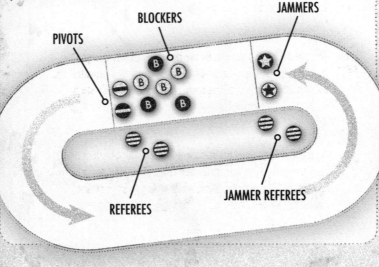

BLOCKERS

JAMMERS

PIVOTS

REFEREES

JAMMER REFEREES